The Day

Whiskey River

Ran Dry

By

Sidney Glaser

ISBN-13: 978-1499538878
ISBN-10: 1499538871

To my wife, Ann,
the wind beneath my wings,
who traipsed all around the world
with me in the pursuit of my dreams,

To Jade and Susan,
unbelievable critics who
encouraged me to
"Git 'er done."

Preface

With the signing of the Treaty of Guadalupe Hidalgo, a small town north of Mexico City, the Mexican-American War came to an end in February 1848. The treaty contained provisions that guaranteed the civil rights of over one hundred thousand Mexicans who chose to remain in the conquered territory. Key to the provisions was the retention of ownership of lands acquired by those Mexicans through Spanish land grants.

About that same time the discovery of gold in California led to a massive migration of Americans to the West, which in turn led to a complete disregard of the treaty by the new settlers. For the Mexicans who remained, their lands and ways of life came under attack by the wave of new settlers and the treaty guarantees were largely ignored. This violation of the treaty fueled decades of conflict over ownership of the land and only those with the economic resources to endure the lengthy litigations that ensued were successful in retaining ownership.

There were some disputes, however, that were settled by alternative measures, well outside the legal arena, that were far more effective than any verdict handed down by an arbitrator or a judge.

This story is about one such dispute.

Chapter One

There was something unique about Whiskey River. In an era when towns were springing up all over the West, the population of Whiskey River neither grew nor declined. Newcomers were discouraged from settling there and the old-timers were compelled to stay by a force that no one was eager to talk about. A substantial number of the ones who fled departed in a pine box. The train, one of the few transportation options, ceased to run on any kind of schedule and rarely stopped at Whiskey River. On the rare occasion it did, it caused more speculation than a pregnant spinster. Once the silver mines gave out, it was simply a matter of time before the railroad curtailed its service including the telegraph, leaving Whiskey River just the way most of the residents wanted it, isolated and uninviting. But all of that changed one day when three raucous blasts from a Great Western locomotive announced its intention to honor Whiskey River with what might become its last ever visit.

As if someone had yelled "free gold," the patrons of Fred Henderson's Emporium abandoned their shopping and spilled out into the bright sunlight to join the rest of the citizens emerging from the false-front building lining both sides of the street. They made their way to where Main Street crossed the tracks, every eye on the iron horse snorting steam as it slowed to a crawl. After all, they couldn't let anyone disembark with the notion they were welcome.

In the Pearly Gate Saloon, the bartender watched Sam Hardin's two hired guns toss their cards on the table and swagger through the batwing doors to take in the scene from the shade of the verandah. Instead of stopping, the train simply slowed down enough for the conductor to pitch two duffel bags from the vestibule of the first coach. As the train started to pick up speed, the onlookers looked on in disbelief as he followed this up by booting a passenger off with the same gusto as his baggage.

"This is as far as you go, bum. Next time I see you, you better have some money if you want to ride this train," the conductor shouted from the steps as the train continued to roll out of town.

"The next time I see you, it'll be at your ma and pa's wedding, you peckerwood," the passenger yelled back.

Doc Carver leaned back in his swivel chair, a glass of whiskey in one hand and a medical journal in the other. The journal reminded him who he was and the whiskey helped him forget. At the sound of the train pulling in, his pale blue eyes drifted to the side window and a clear view of two rucksacks and a body landing in a heap. He drained the glass in one swallow and immediately shifted his glance to his black bag on the desk. Like so many times before, the brief episode meant strangers and strangers invariably meant trouble.

By the time the last coach disappeared over the horizon, just about the whole town had assembled along the south side of the tracks. They watched in stony silence, wondering what to make of the lanky stranger who lay motionless on the ground. Eventually he struggled to his feet and a murmur rose from the onlookers. He was mid to late twenties, about six feet, with sandy hair, steel gray eyes and a ready smile. In fact his boyish good looks and composure belied his apparent impoverished state. When he finished slapping the dust from his clothes with his battered hat, a breeze kicked up a dust devil that sent a tumbleweed chasing after the train, likewise shaking the dust of Whiskey River.

Ever since Sam Hardin took over the largest spread in the area and appointed himself the town leader, he made it his mission to dissuade strangers from settling there backed by the majority of the residents. It was a fact the townspeople didn't much care for Hardin, and one couldn't help but wonder what strange alliance bound them together.

Hardin, a heavy set man with a well tanned face framed by a close cropped, salt and pepper beard, moved to the front of the crowd. Bushy eyebrows made his dark eyes even more ominous.

Sam Hardin cleared his throat and the gathering fell silent. Those nearest him edged away.

"It's plain to see you didn't plan to stop here. Make sure you don't plan to stay."

The stranger shot Hardin a self-conscious grin, removed his hat and bowed with a sweeping gesture. With a nod toward the tumbleweed bouncing along behind the train, he said, "I don't rightly know that I have any plans. Just like that tumbleweed, I go where the wind takes me." He took a step to collect his bags, grimaced, grabbed his ankle and collapsed in a heap. With an apologetic look he said, "I reckon all I'll be doing for a while is just that . . . tumbling on this busted ankle."

In an even more menacing tone, Sam Hardin said, "Son, let me give you a piece of advice." The words said advice, but the tone said ultimatum. "I suggest you give some serious thought to moving on. We don't cotton to drifters and troublemakers. Besides, it's obvious you're out of money and there ain't no work for you here. We're just a bunch of ranchers and sodbusters scratching out a living. What good land there is, it's all taken. The rest, all it's good for is sagebrush and cactus, and ain't no one figured out yet how to make a living from that."

The stranger nodded and said, "I appreciate the advice, but just the same, I don't think I'll be going anywhere on this ankle. If I'd been smart, I would've waited until the train stopped before getting myself throwed off. If you got anybody here calls himself a doctor, I'd sure like him to take a look at my leg."

"We got a doctor . . .leastways what used to be one, but there ain't no place where you can stay."

Jake Morgan, a man with broad shoulders and massive arms, stood in the door of the livery stable taking it all in. He and Sam Hardin weren't enemies, but the last thing you would call them was friends. He and Doc Carver were the only two people in Whiskey River who didn't share Sam Hardin's opinions, of himself or anything else. Doc Carver preferred to keep his sentiments to himself, but Morgan was seldom shy about speaking his mind and never missed a chance to let Hardin know what he was thinking.

Morgan covered the distance from the livery to the train tracks with surprising speed and agility for a man of his size. He studied the face of the newcomer then thrust out a large, meaty hand. "Jake Morgan. I got a place where you can stay in the livery until your ankle's fit. But first, we'll have Doc Carver take a look at it. He stays likkered up most of the time, but he's still one helluva doctor."

The stranger examined the outthrust hand. "Scott Martin. Much obliged. I'd appreciate it if you wouldn't break my fingers in that bear trap. A bad leg's all I can handle at the moment."

They shook hands and Jake hefted the two duffel bags like they were goose down pillows and started for the livery with Scott hobbling along.

Sam Hardin growled at Morgan, "You make sure he's gone when his ankle's mended."

Morgan stopped in his tracks, wheeled and cocked his head to one side. "Or what?"

Hardin glowered at Morgan then shot a glance at the two gunslingers lazing on the porch of the Pearly Gate Saloon. Morgan shrugged and turned away. Scott Martin pretended not to notice the two gunmen, but from under the brim of his hat, he studied them carefully.

Chapter Two

Morgan dropped the two bags just inside the door of a sparsely furnished room adjacent to what barely passed for an office. There was a bunk under the window with a ladder-back chair and a washstand "completing the ensemble." Aside from a porcelain pitcher and bowl on the washstand, the room was as empty as a pauper's purse. The window, with a bleached flour sack for a curtain, looked out on the grassy expanse that separated the livery from Jake's house, a good hundred yards away.

"Hope this suits you. It's not fancy, but it's clean. The outhouse is in the back and a thunder jug is under the bed in case you get a call during the night. I usually get two bits a day for this, but I expect if you had any money, you'd still be on that train. So, you know anything about horses and cleaning stables?"

"Reckon I do. My folks were farmers and we had a small place with some mules and a couple of horses. I've pitched my share of hay."

"Well, then, looks like we're going to come out even. You get this room with meals, and I get myself a stable hand. Any questions?"

Scott nodded, "Yeah, where can I find this Doc Carver? I'd like him to take a look at my foot."

"If he ain't at the Pearly Gate Saloon, you'll find him at his house, last one at the end of the street, directly across from the saloon. The only time he wouldn't be at either one would be when he's making a call, but I saw his buggy in the back of his house, so I know he's in town. Want me to go with you?"

Scott shook his head. "I can manage."

"Well, I guess that's it then, unless you have any more questions."

"Just one. Who was that jasper that went out of his way to make me feel so welcome?"

Morgan snorted, "Sam Hardin. Owns most of the good land around these parts. Thinks he owns the town too."

"Nobody seemed in a hurry to disagree with him," Scott said. "What are they afraid of?"

"What makes you think people are afraid of him?" Jake asked.

"The way they backed up when he took over. How no one interrupted or said anything. It was pretty obvious to me."

"Let's just say it doesn't pay to cross him, and leave it at that," Jake said indicating the conversation was over.

Scott, however, was insistent. "Those two hombres hanging out at the saloon wouldn't have anything to do with it, would they?"

Morgan squinted at Martin. "You don't miss much do you?"

"I try not to, but you still haven't answered my question. Why are they so afraid of him?"

"Look, son, it ain't none of your business and you best leave it that way. Your ankle should be better in a few days and by then you'll be long gone. Why get involved?"

Scott gave him a mischievous grin. "Oh, I don't know. Seems like a pretty nice town. I might get to like it here. I figure if I'm going to stay, I ought to learn as much as I can about Whiskey River."

"You've already learned all you need to know. One, you ain't wanted here and two, Sam Hardin has two very persuasive friends to make sure you get the message."

"I can be pretty persuasive myself," Scott said in a quiet voice.

·   ·   ·   ·   ·

As soon as Jake had left, Scott explored the livery and checked out the horses in the stables. The animals were quality stock and well cared for. Unlike most blacksmiths, Jake kept his place neat and clean, especially the tool shed and tack room. Back in a corner Scott found a broken pitchfork handle from which he fashioned a cane and struck out for Doc Carver's house.

Across from the livery sat the bank and next to that the freight and stagecoach depot. Several houses farther down at the end of the street was Doc Carver's place. Sandwiched between the depot and Doc Carver's at the end of the street were a few small shops and the town meeting hall. Scott deemed it prudent to avoid any confrontation with Hardin's hired guns, so he hobbled across the street toward the bank. The street was deserted, but he could feel the stares from behind the curtained windows as he continued on toward Doc Carver's.

What in tarnation is going on here? What are they afraid of?

On the other side, at the north end, was the Emporium, separated by an alley from the Pearly Gate Saloon. Curiously, whether by design or by chance, the town carpenter and casket maker's place was right next to the saloon. Immediately after that was a pretentious building with gold lettering in a window that proclaimed it to be Sam Hardin's place of business. Between Hardin's place and the livery there was a seamstress, the barbershop, and a scattering of nondescript false front stores, just like most of the towns out West that sprang up until the silver or gold petered out.

He suddenly found himself in front of Doc Carver's place and rapped on the door with his makeshift cane.

"The door's open. Come on in," a voice rasped.

Doc Carver, as disheveled as the recluse drunk Jake described him, spun his swivel chair away from the window and studied his visitor over wire-rimmed glasses. He cocked his head to one side and said, "How do you expect to pay me when you don't have enough money for train fare?"

Scott threw his head back and laughed. "So you caught the performance this morning?"

Doc nodded. "Yep, that was quite a show. Just throw your foot up here on the desk and I'll slip off that boot."

Scott groaned when Doc tugged on the boot and winced when he removed his sock.

"Hmm, no discoloration, no swelling. Tell me if this hurts."

Scott let out a yell when Doc squeezed a spot just below the ankle.

"Now, close your eyes and tell me if it hurts here."

Doc scarcely brushed his finger on the protrusion of the anklebone and Scott almost jumped out of his chair.

"Just what I thought," he said. He poured himself a glass of whiskey and one for Scott.

"Here, drink this. It ain't for the pain, it's to help wash down the bad news I got for you. I'm afraid this is going to cost you more than I thought."

Scott looked at him quizzically. "It's that bad, huh?"

"It's got nothing to do with your ankle. I imagine if you want everybody to think it's busted, it's worth something for me to keep my mouth shut."

"Now why would I want to do something like that?"

"I don't know, but you must have your reasons. Whatever it is, let's drink to it. There's damn little else to drink to."

Scott tossed down the whiskey, made a wry face and asked, "What's going on in this town? Except for Jake and you, seems like everybody wants me gone, and I'm not sure about you."

"Doesn't make snake shit to me you stay or you go. You stay you're dead. You go, you don't find out what you came here for."

"Who says I came here for anything? It's pure coincidence I landed here."

"What's your name?"

"Scott Martin."

"Well, Scott, come over here and look over my shoulder through that window."

Scott circled the desk and peered through the open window. "Now what?"

"Just wanted to show you what a fine doctor I am. Noticed you didn't even limp coming around this desk."

"You s-o-n-n-u-v-a bitch," Scott drew out.

"A bigger sonnuva bitch than you think. From this spot right here I could see you throw your bags from the train right before you jumped. How much did you have to pay the conductor to act like he threw you off?"

Scott rolled his eyes. "Probably a lot less than you're going to charge me to forget you saw it."

Doc Carver poured himself another shot. "Forgetting ain't what I do best."

Chapter Three

Back at the livery Scott unpacked his two bags. In the top drawer of the washstand he stashed his gun belt and pistol under his shirts and underwear. After he re-assembled his Winchester, he stood it in the corner, and in the bottom drawer, under the rest of his things, he placed a Bowie knife that had belonged to his father, or so his mother said. He didn't remember how he came by it, he just remembered always having it. Next to the knife he carefully placed a gold watch that his mother said belonged to a distant uncle she hardly knew. Finally, he removed his money belt with five hundred dollars in gold coins and placed it in the thunder jug under the bed. He didn't believe anyone was brave enough to look there nor think him dumb enough to hide anything in it. He hastily closed both drawers at a knock on the door.

He crossed the room slowly, his makeshift cane tapping out a slow cadence, and opened the door to a vision with dark eyes that matched her long black hair tied with a blue ribbon at the back. Her blue plaid blouse, tucked snugly into a tan suede riding skirt and open at the neck, left very little to the imagination.

In contrast to the icon of gentility and beauty, the vision spoke with the authority of a ranch foreman. "Hello, I'm Laura Randle.

Jake said you'd be staying a while, so I brought a towel, a blanket and some linens."

Scott, astonished at the sight of such a stunning woman, groped for a reply.

Laura's brow furrowed. "Are you all right?"

"Yes, yes, fine. It's just . . . I wasn't expecting . . . I mean I thought it was Jake, not someone as pretty as you."

Laura's cheeks reddened through her deep tan, but she smiled appreciatively.

"Jake also said you hurt your leg, so I'll be glad to fix the bed for you, if you like."

"No, no. Thanks. I can manage. It's just my ankle."

Laura deposited the linens on the bunk, surveyed the room and started for the door. With her hand on the knob she turned and said, "Mrs. Morgan said to tell you dinner's at five. I'd advise you to be on time. She gets mighty peeved when the food sits out and gets cold."

Scott thrust out his hand. "Scott Martin. Thanks. You tell Mrs. Morgan I won't let her dinner get cold."

Laura took the outstretched hand. Her firm grip belied the softness of her hand. "See you at dinner."

Scott watched as she retreated toward the house, the fringes of her skirt swaying to the rhythmic motion of her hips.

Dang, now there's another reason I might want to hang around Whiskey River.

·   ·   ·   ·   ·

The Morgan house, set in the shade of a patch of cottonwood trees, was no more than two spits and a stone's throw away, but with the cane and the fake limp, it seemed much farther. "But I have to keep up appearances," Scott figured. The frilly curtains in the windows, the flower baskets hanging on the front porch, and the vegetable garden on the side were definitely a woman's touch. "But whose," Scott wondered, "Mrs. Morgan's or Laura's."

Laura met him at the door and took his hat. "Well, a man of his word. Right on time."

She led him to the spacious kitchen where a table had been set across the room from the wood-burning stove to escape its heat.

Mrs. Morgan gave an *olla* one last stir with a long wooden spoon and wiped her hands on her apron. She greeted Scott with a warm smile. "I am Teresa." She used the Spanish pronunciation, Tay-ress-ah. "*Mi casa es su casa*, as my people say."

"My house is your house," Laura translated.

"Thank you. Very kind of you. So, I take it you're Spanish."

"No, I am not. I am American."

Scott flushed. "I'm sorry. I meant your heritage is Spanish."

"No, that is not what you meant, but I admire your quickness. You should be a lawyer."

Scott gulped.

"What's the matter? Did I trip on a sensitive word?" Teresa asked enjoying Scott's discomfiture.

"No . . . no . . . not at all. I just wonder what in the world a lawyer would do in Whiskey River."

"Put that scoundrel Sam Hardin in Jail is what," Jake boomed as he came through the back door carrying an armload of firewood.

"Enough of that, Jake. Let's get to the table," Teresa said with a barely perceptible nod toward Laura.

Jake pronounced the blessing and started passing the steaming bowls of rice, pinto beans, and *chiles rellenos.*

Teresa handed Scott a plate of hot corn tortillas wrapped in a cloth to keep them warm.

"Thank you. Ah, tortillas. I haven't had any in a long time. I love Mexican food."

Teresa fixed him with an icy stare. "This is not Mexican food."

Scott made a hopeless gesture and looked to Laura for help.

Laura smiled in amusement.

"I'm sorry. It . . . it all looks the same to me," Scott stammered.

"Well, it may look the same, but it's quite different. It's what we call Northern New Mexico, a combination of Spanish, Mexican, and Anasazi cooking."

"I hope I don't sound ignorant, but what is Anasazi?"

Laura rescued him from his embarrassment. "They are the Indians who lived on these lands before the Navajos and Apaches."

Jake broke the awkward silence that ensued. "I see you've met Laura. You're probably wondering who she is and why she's staying here, right?"

"Well, yes, I mean no. I mean I haven't really given it much thought. What I really mean is her name is Randle and yours is Morgan and you all can't be related, or am I putting my foot in my mouth again?"

"You certainly have a talent for that," Teresa said.

Jake reached for another helping of the *chiles rellenos*. "You're right, we're not related. Seems like we're in the habit of picking up strays, except this one didn't get thrown off a train. She came voluntarily."

Scott started to say something, but Jake cut him short. "I think it's only fair to tell you that Sam Hardin is her stepfather."

Scott ran his hand through his hair. *"What in the hell's going on in this town?"*

After dinner Jake and Scott sat on the porch rocking their beans and rice while Teresa and Laura cleaned up. With each puff Jake's pipe glowed like the forge in his blacksmith shop. When he started sucking air, he tapped out the ashes, put the pipe in the pocket of his bib overalls and quietly asked, "What did Doc Carver say about your ankle?"

Scott hesitated, wondering how strongly Doc Carver observed physician/patient confidentiality. Would he blab what he knew to Jake, or anyone else for that matter?

After all, how far can you trust a drunk? And Jake . . . how does he fit in? Obviously no friend of Hardin, yet his stepdaughter is living with him.

On the other hand, he'd need an ally to find what he came here for, and Jake seemed to be his best bet at the moment. Should he share his reason for coming to Whiskey River? Could he trust Jake Morgan? All of this whirled through his mind in the five or six seconds it took him to respond.

"Doc says it should be good as new in a week or so."

"So, that means you'll be hanging around for a spell. Think you can fork a saddle?"

"I reckon. It's my ankle, not my backside that got hurt."

"Good. Then you can accompany me to a Navajo pueblo where I do some horse trading. In the morning we'll load up the buckboard with some supplies from Henderson's and head out from there. It's a two day ride. I'll drive the wagon. You can saddle up the paint."

"Are those Navajos friendly?"

"Not to most white folks. Me, I get along with them. I treat them square and they respect me for that. How do you feel about them?"

Scott shrugged. "Pretty much the same way. I knew one growing up . . . well a half-breed . . . when I was little. He tried to live in the white man's world, but he never was happy. Eventually went back to his people . . . somewhere here in New Mexico. I lost track of him. Maybe I'll ask around and see if anyone's heard of him."

Jake took out his pipe and fired up a new load of tobacco. He rocked back and forth a few times as if in deep thought. Abruptly he said, "How come you haven't asked about Laura? I figured you'd at least be curious why she's living with us when it's obvious her stepfather and I don't see eye to eye."

The sudden shift in the conversation caught Scott by surprise. "I don't reckon it's any of my business. If you feel I should know more than what you told me, then you'd let me know."

Jake blew a cloud of smoke toward the ceiling. "Seems to me you'd like to make it your business."

"What do you mean by that?"

"I noticed the way you were looking at her tonight."

Chapter Four

Laura watched from the porch as Jake led the team from the stable and hitched it to the buckboard. Right behind, Scott emerged leading the pinto, jet black with white splotches. He gave the saddle cinch one last tug, lowered the stirrup and mounted. On an impulse he looked back toward the house and couldn't suppress a wide grin when Laura waved and flashed him a dazzling smile. He touched his fingers to the brim of his hat and smiled even more broadly.

"Are you going to just sit there and gawk at her, or are you ready to ride?"

Scott felt the color rush to his face. "Just being neighborly." Maybe he was reading more than he should have into Laura's smile, but it sure did seem to him a lot more than a friendly gesture. He waved back and touched his spurs to the horse's flanks. Laura walked to the front gate and followed him with her eyes until the two men reached the Emporium.

"He sure cuts a handsome figure. Sits that saddle like it was made for him."

Laura's cheeks reddened and without turning her head said to Teresa, "You think so? I really didn't take notice. I was just enjoying the cool morning air."

"That wasn't all you were enjoying, girl. Aren't many good looking men like him in these parts."

Laura shrugged. "If you say so."

"I'd say so, and not rough around the edges like most of the ranch hands around here."

With a toss of her head Laura said, "Like I said, I didn't pay that much attention to him."

"Well, you sure paid a lot of attention to him last night. It was shameful the way you flirted with him."

"Just being polite, after all, he was our guest."

"I can't say I blame you though. He is a decent sort, but you know what . . . there's something familiar about him, or at least he reminds me of somebody."

With a devilish look Laura said, "Don't tell me you're getting ideas about him."

Teresa gave her a playful whack on the setter. "Get yourself back to the house and help clean up the mess those two left."

· · · · ·

Whiskey River came to life slowly every morning, and not much happened during the rest of the day to speed up the process. The life signs, while recognizable, usually went unnoticed. Fred Henderson opened the Emporium promptly at seven, probably the biggest event of the day, just one notch ahead of the ritual emptying of the cuspidors from the Pearly Gate Saloon. Along with the spittle and tobacco juice, it wasn't uncommon to find false teeth, spectacles and other items of a personal nature.

Today promised to be livelier. When Henderson arrived, he found Jake and Scott waiting with their list of supplies . . . a bolt of material, some tools, high crown hats, and a whole lot of trinkets. Jake sent Scott to the Pearly Gate to buy a case of whiskey while he loaded the buckboard. When the horse trading reached a stalemate, even a bottle of the worst imitation of rye whiskey man ever created had a way of clearing the air and breaking the impasse.

Scott gimped his way next door to the saloon and pushed through the swinging doors. He paused to let his eyes adjust to the dim interior while J. D. MacPhearson, owner and bartender, mopped the floor with a strong mixture of water and pine oil to camouflage the stench of stale smoke and spilled beer. He looked up when Scott said, "Jake Morgan wants a case of whiskey, the cheapest you got, and says to put it on his tab."

Mac acknowledged Scott with a nod and a grunt before he disappeared around the bar. It was only then that Scott saw Hardin's two weasels sprawled at a table in a corner to his right.

"Whooeee! What is that smell, Marvin?"

"Smells like horse piss mixed with mule shit to me, Snake."

"Where do you reckon it's coming from?"

"I didn't smell nothing 'til that shit shoveler walked in."

Scott tightened his grip on the makeshift cane and limped to the bar.

"Hey, stable boy, does shoveling shit make you hard of hearing, or are you just plain stupid?"

Scott turned halfway around and leaned back against the bar to face his tormentors. He rested his right elbow on the bar and slid his hand under his jacket where his Bowie knife, jammed in his waistband, pressed against the small of his back. He cupped his other hand to his left ear and said, "Sorry, I don't seem to hear you. Working for a living seems to do that to a person."

Their grins turned into sneers. They both got to their feet, adjusted their holsters and swaggered to the bar. They stopped in front of Scott, their feet spread and their gun hands brushing the butts of their pistols. Not more than five feet separated them.

MacPhearson hefted the box of whiskey, set it on the bar and said, "Now boys, let's not have any trouble. It's too damned early in the morning for that. Besides, I just got done cleaning up this side of the place," and went back to his mopping.

The one called Snake, his wiry body tensed like a cougar ready to pounce, kept flexing the fingers of his right hand. "Ain't going to be no trouble, Mac. Just going to clean up the air in here a mite."

His sidekick, Marv, searched Scott with his bloodshot eyes for a gun.

"You and your stink are making it hard to breathe in here," Snake said. "If you know what's good for you, you'll just leave that whiskey on the bar and vamoose."

Scott feigned surprise. "Doggone, this is a right unfriendly town. A man can't even buy himself a drink of whiskey without some jasper telling him he ain't welcome."

"It ain't the town, shit shoveler. It's you. You smelling up the place, now git."

"Seems to me a man's got a right to spend his money where he pleases without two dung balls like you butting in."

Marv's eyes widened a fraction of a second before his hand moved toward his gun, warning enough for Scott to bring up his cane sharply up into Marv's crotch and whip his knife out of its scabbard. Marv fell to the floor clutching his vitals.

Snake's gun had hardly cleared the holster when the point of Scott's knife found itself embedded in that delicate area where Snake's thighs joined his body. Shock was the prominent of his reactions along with the fury at being outdrawn, by a knife at that.

Scott, his face no more than a foot from Snake's said in a quiet voice, "Don't even think about lifting that gun unless you want to spend the rest or your life singing in an all girl's choir."

Snake's stare was venomous . . . probably how he got his nickname. "This ain't over stable boy. You better get yourself a gun, 'cause next time we meet you're going to need one."

"Don't need a gun to kill a snake. But, if you insist, release the hammer on that smoke pole of yours and drop it on the floor."

Snake continued to glare at Scott, his eyes filled with rage at the ultimate humiliation of letting someone take his gun away, but did what he was told. Scott picked it up and shoved it in his waistband.

In that instant Jake pushed through the swinging doors. "What's happening with the whiskey? I'm all loaded up and ready to pull . . ."

He stared incredulously at one gunman on floor massaging his crotch and the other one being held at knifepoint. "What in the hell?"

Scott put the knife back in its sheath. "Just a little unfriendly argument. I believe I won."

●　　●　　●　　●　　●

With Scott on the paint and Jake in the wagon, they headed northeast in the direction of the Sangre de Cristo mountains, which took them past Sam Hardin's spread. Scott hesitated a moment and took a good, long look at the main house, an imposing structure set back about two hundred yards from the road.

"Now, just why would Laura Randle give up a mansion like this to live with the Morgans?"

The team fell into an easy gait with Scott taking the point. They rode in silence for three hours until Jake pulled up to rest the horses in a clump of willows near a stream. Scott loosened the saddle cinch and joined Jake in the shade of a cottonwood for a lunch of biscuits, venison jerky, and some pinto beans from the previous night.

When the utensils had been cleaned and stowed, Jake lit up his pipe. He leaned back against the tree trunk and asked, "What happened back there in the saloon?"

Scott shrugged. "Not much. We just exchanged unpleasantries."

"So, how come one of them ends up on the floor grabbing at his crotch, and the other one on the wrong end of a pig sticker?"

"Well, the one called Snake and I were having a discussion that was getting a bit testy, when the other one made a move for his gun. I put my hands up to show him I wasn't armed, but I forgot I was holding onto my cane, and it came up and whacked him good right in the biscuits. When Snake saw his partner go down like a roped calf, he went for his gun, but by that time I had my knife in his most sensitive area. He wasn't that eager to hand over his pistol when I asked him to, but by that time I guess he figured he'd run out of options. That's when you showed up."

"Well, Scott, it don't make no difference who said what to who, or who started it. You humiliated them and their kind ain't likely to forget it."

"Seems like nobody does a lot of forgetting around here."

"What's that supposed to mean?"

"Nothing . . . just something Doc Carver said yesterday. But, that spread outside of town, that's Hardin's right?"

"Yep, that's the one, the Lazy-H."

"Looks like it's worth a lot of money. How did he come by a place like that?"

"It's a long story, Scott. Tie the pony to the back of the wagon and set beside me. I'll tell you on the way."

Chapter Five

Sam Hardin stuck his head in the door of the Pearly Gate and called to MacPhearson. "If you see Snake Weston and that idiot sidekick of his, you tell them I want to see them, pronto."

"They were here earlier, but they lit out like scalded hogs right after their quarrel with that feller that Jake took in," MacPhearson said without looking up from the glasses he was wiping.

"What feller . . . you mean that drifter that came in on the train yesterday?"

MacPhearson nodded. "That's the one. He might be just a tumbleweed like he says, but I'll tell you one thing, he's sure got sand. Your two guys were riding him pretty hard and he just smiled at them and gave them as good as he was getting. Then before you know it, Culpepper's on the floor holding his nuts and Snake is minus one gun."

Hardin's eyebrows shot up. "You saying he took Snake's gun off him?"

"That's right. Snake didn't have much choice. It was either that or get his balls lopped off."

"What the hell you talking about? Lopped off."

"That's what I said. That feller whipped out a knife the fastest I ever saw and before Snake could even clear his holster, he had it jammed up his crotch."

Hardin looked bewildered. "When did all this happen?"

"Right after I opened up, that jasper came in here for some whiskey Jake Morgan sent him for. Seems like them two are heading up Santa Fe way to do some horse trading. Anyway, Snake and Culpepper start riding him pretty hard, but he still keeps his cool. The next thing I know Culpepper goes for his gun and the stranger whacks him right in the biscuits with his cane. By the time Snake realizes what's going on . . . well, I already told you the rest of it."

Sam Hardin's eyes narrowed. "You mean to tell me that a man with a busted ankle and nothing but a knife, sends one of them sprawling and disarms the other one."

"That's exactly the way it was."

Hardin, his eyes now mere slits said, "You see them, tell 'em to get their asses to my office."

•   •   •   •   •

Jake tapped his pipe on the side of the buckboard and scattered the ashes with the toe of his boot. Scott tied the paint to the buckboard and took a seat alongside Jake. "You said you'd tell me about the Hardin place. I'm listening."

Jake eyed Scott suspiciously. "How come you so interested in Hardin?"

"Just curious is all. I was wondering how he got to be the big man around town?"

Jake popped the reins and the two-horse team leaned into the harness. He looked straight ahead and spoke in a monotone, like he was reciting a history lesson. "About thirty years ago Whiskey River was nothing more than a stagecoach stop. A place where the driver could rest the horses and the passengers could spend the night. Then they started mining silver and the place grew to a pretty good size town. That's when the railroad started regular service."

"Excuse me for interrupting, but how did it get the name of Whiskey River?"

"Like I said, things were booming here and in all the dance halls and saloons that sprung up, they said the whiskey flowed like a river. The name stuck, but the silver mines eventually gave out and the train seldom stopped, so folks turned to farming and raising cattle."

"It was mostly open range, but people started staking claims to sizeable chunks of land. Since nobody disputed them, they eventually became owners claiming squatters' rights, or something like that. However, there was one ranch that a Martinez family owned under a Spanish land grant. It was the biggest and best spread in the territory."

"So what happened to them . . . the Martinez's?" Scott asked.

"Hold your water. I'm getting to that. Sam Hardin always had his eye on that piece of property and would have married the devil's bastard daughter to get it. When the last of the Martinez family got hurt in a cattle stampede, Sam Hardin thought for sure he was finally going to get his hands on it. He went to see the dying man about buying it, but to his surprise, this Martinez had left the property to a niece somewhere back East."

"How did that set with Hardin?"

"He was madder than a wild boar. Went all the way to Santa Fe to challenge the land grant, but legally there was nothing he could do. The land rightfully belonged to his niece, Sarah Chandler, who was living in Kansas City."

"So what happened to the land?"

"The niece and her husband, Jesse Chandler, moved out here to settle. Of course by the time they got here the place had run down some and a good bit of the cattle was gone. Some say run off, but more'n likely they was long roped by Sam Hardin."

"Long roped?" Scott said with a puzzled look.

"That's cowboy lingo for rustling."

"Is there anything Sam Hardin won't do to get his way?" Scott wondered aloud.

"Like I said yesterday, he's a man you don't want to cross."

"So, what happened to the Chandlers?"

"It took them five years, but they did a fine job of rebuilding the place. Teresa, my wife, and Sarah became good friends, what with both of them being of Spanish descent, and Sarah confessed to her that she wanted to start a family. Wanted someone to leave the place to, not like her uncle who had nobody. Gossip had it that Jesse didn't want children, but either that was pure hogwash, or somebody slipped up, because after five years Sarah gives birth to a boy and everybody's happy. Six years later, for reasons nobody knows yet, Sarah picks up and goes back East with her son and an orphan whose mother was a Navajo and the father a white man. Only the mother knew who he was, but she just took off without revealing who the daddy was."

"But that doesn't explain how Hardin got the ranch."

"That's the part I'm getting to. I guess Jesse expected Sarah to come back, but when she didn't, he took to drinking and gambling. He ended up owing money to everybody, but mostly to Sam Hardin. One night in the Pearly Gate Saloon, Jesse was drunk as usual playing poker. People say it was the biggest pot they'd ever seen, and when Jesse turned over his cards and started raking in the money, the dude you had a run in with this morning, Snake, accused him of cheating and shot him. He claimed Jesse went for a Derringer that was tucked in his waistband."

"Was that true?"

"Well, he did have a gun, but folks believe Snake's sidekick, Marvin Culpepper, planted it on him when he checked to see if he was dead. The truth is, in all the time people knew Jesse Chandler, he was never, ever known to carry a gun."

"What became of Chandler?" Scott asked with an edge to his voice.

"Nobody knows. He managed to get on his horse and ride out, and hasn't been seen since. When it looked like Chandler wasn't ever coming back, Hardin seized the ranch. He said it was in payment of Chandler's debts. There were other people that Chandler owed money to and they were set to challenge Hardin's claim to the ranch. The word is Hardin gave each one of them a parcel of two hundred acres of land to drop their claims."

"If he bought them off to keep their mouths shut, how come he needs those two hired guns?" Scott asked.

"It turns out that these two hombres, Snake and Marv, were working for Hardin long before Chandler was shot, and there was speculation that Hardin hired them, specifically to get rid of Chandler. Even so, a couple of the people who weren't happy with the way the land was split up and wanted a bigger chunk, threatened to see the U.S. Marshal in Santa Fe. However, before they had the chance, they ended up dead in a shoot-out with Snake. That put an end to the grumbling. All of a sudden everybody seemed happy with the way the land was divided up."

"It certainly sounds like those two were working for Hardin before Chandler was shot. How long ago did all this take place?"

"Oh, about fifteen or sixteen years ago. Why?"

"Then, why's he still need those two?"

With a hapless expression Jake said, "I guess blackmail works both ways."

Chapter Six

Sam Hardin sat at his massive oak desk piercing the two men standing before him with his most contemptuous look. Marv Culpepper shuffled his feet in awkward silence. Snake Weston tried to hide his chagrin behind his usual sneer. Hardin's eyes darted to Snake's empty holster then back to his face, a pathetic portrait of embarrassment.

"If you two ain't the sorriest excuse for gunfighters I have ever seen. It's going to be a long time before folks around here forget how a half crippled saddle tramp got the best of you with nothing but a makeshift cane and a knife. The worst part is you make me look just as dumb for hiring you."

Hardin's piercing stare demanded a reply. Marv, as usual, deferred to his partner, content to follow his lead.

Snake simply shrugged. "We were just having a little fun. Anyway, you made it clear to that stable hand yesterday he wasn't welcome here and we thought we'd just reinforce the message. After all that's what you're paying us for, ain't it?"

"I'm not paying you to look stupid. His ankle will be mended soon enough and he'll be long gone from here. Why get his curiosity up?"

"I just wanted to make sure he'll be gone. Who knows, he might decide to light here a spell and then we'll really have to take care of him."

"Like you took care of him this morning?"

Snake stiffened and his eyes hardened. "He just got lucky. If it hadn't been for Marv distracting me, he'd be lying in a pine box right now."

"The way I hear it, luck had nothing to do with it. The next time you tangle with that feller, you better make sure you get the drop on him. He looks like he could be trouble."

Snake jammed his hat on his head and said, "The next time is going to be his last time."

Hardin scoffed, "And just how you planning to do that without your gun?"

•   •   •   •   •

There was about an hour of daylight left when Jake reined in the horses alongside a stream where they made camp for the night. Between tending to the horses and fixing supper, there wasn't time for talk, but once the last cup of coffee was poured and the dregs tossed on the fire, the conversation turned back to Sam Hardin.

"What about Mrs. Chandler? How did he explain things to her?" Scott asked.

"He packed up Jesse's belongings and shipped them back to her along with a letter, so he says, informing her that he was the new owner of the ranch."

"So that was it. Chandler gets killed and Hardin takes over the spread. And Mrs. Chandler does nothing?"

"Son it's more complicated than that. Don't know why I'm telling you all this. You'll be gone from here soon enough and Whiskey River will be long forgotten. But, since you asked, about two years after Sarah Chandler left, Hardin married Abigail Randle, a widow with a four year old daughter, Laura. That was just about two years before Jesse got shot."

"What's that got to do with the Chandlers?"

"Practically everything. A year after they married, Abigail realized she'd made a big mistake and they started sleeping in separate bedrooms. In a small place like this you can't keep something like that a secret. Before you know it the whole town knew about it, and when Abigail turns up pregnant, everybody's wondering who the daddy is, but they were either too polite or too scared to mention it. Teresa and Abigail were friendly, but not that close. That's why she was surprised as all get out when Abigail asked her to take Laura if anything happened to her. Teresa said it was like she had a premonition that something terrible was going to happen."

"So, what did happen?"

"She and the baby died in childbirth." Jake gave Scott a baleful look and continued. "According to the rumors she 'fell' causing her to go into premature labor. The Mexican housekeeper said she was in terrible pain, screaming at Harding to fetch Doc Carver. By the time Hardin finally agreed to send for Doc, both Abigail and the baby were gone. Doc was drunk as usual when he got there, but there was nothing he could've done anyway. Later he confessed to me that he never saw anybody so banged up from just falling down."

"So what did Hardin say about you and Teresa taking Laura?" Scott asked.

"At first he thought it was a good idea, 'but only until I get over Abigail's passing' he said. That bastard never had any intention of taking her back. He was glad to get rid of her."

"Did Abigail ever say who the daddy . . ."

"You ask too many questions that don't concern you. Douse that fire and get some sleep."

"But, I still don't see what this had to do with the Chandlers."

"That'll have to wait. If we want to get to the pueblo by noon tomorrow, we need to get an early start. Let's get some shuteye."

Chapter Seven

Jake was up at first light and had a fire going before Scott stirred, but it didn't take long for the aroma of fresh coffee and bacon frying to rouse him. Scott fumbled for his boots, slapped them together upside down to evict any scorpions or tarantulas that may have taken up residence in them, and slipped them on. At the stream he splashed his face with the cold water and dried with the tail of his shirt.

"Now I'm ready for some of that hoof-rot medicine you call coffee."

"Got some bacon, eggs and the rest of the biscuits to go with 'em. That about does it for the grub. We'll get some pemmican from the Indians and maybe shoot a rabbit or squirrel on the way back."

Scott rubbed his belly. "Pemmican, now that's something to look forward to."

They broke camp after breakfast and began the four hour ride to the pueblo.

•   •   •   •   •

On her way to the Emporium to buy a few items for Teresa, Laura stopped at the dressmaker where the news of Scott's run-in with Hardin's toughs was already an hour old. When she got to the Emporium, it was abuzz with the gossip. Everybody in the store had an opinion.

"It's about time those two got their comeuppance. I do declare, the way they strut around like they own the place."

"Well, we all know why Hardin keeps them around."

"You'd think after all this time, no one's going to rock the boat."

"What do we know about that stranger? What if he's worse than that Snake and his crony?"

"I don't know. He looks like he's cut from a different cloth. Seems to be something decent about him, for a drifter that is."

"Do you suppose he's come to Whiskey River to settle a score with them?"

"Not likely, what with the way he was booted from the train. What I figure is Hardin's two hoodlums just picked the wrong man to tangle with."

A new voice said, "Well, I'll say this, it sure is refreshing to know there's one more person in Whiskey River who's not afraid to stand up to them."

All heads snapped in the direction of Laura Randle who had entered unnoticed.

"That's easy for you to say. Your step daddy is the one they work for," said Hester Gladstone, the town biddy with the wattles to match.

"Mrs. Gladstone, you're mistaken if you think that cuts me any slack. He's no more a father to me than that wooden Indian outside," Laura shot back.

"All the same, if it hadn't been for him and those killers he hired, we'd all be a lot better off."

"Mrs. Gladstone, I'm certainly not defending him or anything he's done, but it seems to me, you've all prospered with the land you got because of Sam Hardin. The problem is you're all envious because he's a lot more prosperous."

Hester Gladstone shook her finger in Laura's face. "How dare you talk to us like that. You have no right. And that Jake Morgan, what's he thinking of letting that ruffian stay in our town?"

Laura brushed Hester's hand aside. "Make up your mind. First you're glad somebody stands up to those two, then you want 'that ruffian' run out of town. You made your choices, now live with them. If you're not happy with the choices you made, then do something about it, but don't let me hear you criticizing Teresa and Jake Morgan for your own greed. And one more thing, I don't want to ever hear any of you mention Sam Hardin's name and mine in same breath."

Hester Gladstone wasn't accustomed to anyone talking to her like that and challenging her dictums. Along with the other biddies, she stared in open-mouthed shock as Laura wheeled and strode from the Emporium.

•　　•　　•　　•　　•

The sun was high in the sky when the adobe dwellings of the pueblo peeked over the horizon. Against the sky their earth tones contrasted with the sky blue background, but as Scott and Jake neared, they blended so perfectly with the surrounding terrain, they were hardly visible. The doors, painted a bright blue to keep evil spirits out, provided the only splash of color.

At the sight of a small band of braves riding out to meet them, Jake said, "Stay close to the wagon and let me do the talking. Even though they don't speak a lot of English, they're real good at reading expressions and gestures. So, wear your best poker face."

"What if I don't play poker?"

"You damn well better learn fast."

In response to Scott's quizzical look Jake said, "Some Indians have left the reservation and have been raiding homesteaders and wagon trains. It's got the settlers all riled up and they've got itchy trigger fingers for any Indian they come across. You might say the Indians ain't as friendly as they used to be."

Jake reined in the team and waited. The seven riders approached cautiously, their rifles cradled in their arms. Jake, as motionless as an owl, said in a low voice, "Don't move or even twitch until I say so."

When no more than twenty yards separated them, the riders reined in their mounts.

The one who appeared to be the leader called out, "Morgan, you go back. White man not welcome."

"Soaring Eagle, we come in peace. We come to buy horses."

"Horses for your soldiers to ride against my people?"

Jake, his arms outstretched and palms up, replied, "We are friends. I do not sell horses to people who ride against my friends."

"I am sorry, we do not have horses to sell."

Jake nodded slowly. "I understand how you feel, Soaring Eagle. If I was in your moccasins, I would feel the same way, but we have been friends many years and we have great trust in each other. Can we go to the pueblo and have a drink and talk?"

Scott studied the un-welcoming committee closely as they conferred among themselves. Without taking his eyes off them Jake asked, "What do you make of it?"

"The one on the roan looks like he ain't buying what the rest of them are selling."

"How do you figure that?"

"He seems too adamant."

"Too what?"

"Adamant, you know, stubborn, hard set against it."

"Where'd you learn words like that?"

"I had some school housing."

"So did I, but they never learned me fancy words like that."

Abruptly, the lone dissenter wheeled his mount and took off at a gallop for the pueblo and Soaring Eagle nodded at Jake, "Come we talk."

A stream that ran alongside the pueblo formed one of the boundaries. The adobe dwellings, lined up in a semi-circle formed the other boundary. Between the stream and the dwellings was a large area the Spaniards would have called a plaza. Entrance to the plaza, where the children were playing and dogs wandered about, was through a heavy wood door.

Jake and Scott followed Soaring Eagle and his band through the gate and parked the wagon under some willows at the edge of the stream. Jake unhitched the team and led them to the water where they drank thirstily of the cool, fresh water while Scott unsaddled his mount and removed the bridle. Jake removed two bottles of whiskey from his saddlebag before joining Soaring Eagle in the center of the plaza.

"Soaring Eagle, please accept this small gift as a sign of our friendship."

Soaring Eagle took the two bottles and eyed Scott warily. "You want to loosen my tongue and cloud my brain before we do business."

Jake laughed, "I only give you the whisky. You decide to drink it."

He then grew serious. "This is my partner, Scott Martin. He's a good man. Can, we do business?"

Soaring Eagle, maintaining a stoic air said, "Yes, since the recent trouble, white man does not want to trade with us. Before the white man came we had everything we needed. Now we depend too much on the white man's goods."

Then his eyes narrowed and his face took on a shrewd look. "But don't think we are so desperate we give away our horses."

Jake rolled his eyes. "When did you ever give anything away?"

At the corral the trading was uneventful for the first three animals . . . horses that a cowboy with empty pockets could afford for working cattle, but nothing special beyond that. Jake looked over the remaining horses and asked Soaring Eagle, "Are these all you have?"

Soaring Eagle barked an order to a Navajo youth who disappeared in a cluster of trees and returned leading a handsome dun colored stallion. Jake, uncharacteristic of an experienced horse trader, did a poor job of hiding his excitement. It was not lost on Soaring Eagle and Scott intuited that Jake was not leaving without the dun, and that Soaring Eagle was well aware of it.

Jake walked around the animal a few times and examined it closely before whispering to Scott, "What a beautiful horse! What do you think it'll take to get him?"

Scott kept his voice low. "Pass on it, Jake. It's damaged goods."

Jake's jaw went slack. "How do you . . . what the hell you mean by that?"

Scott took Jake aside. "I speak a little Navajo. Your pal, Soaring Eagle, told the kid that went to fetch it to bring out the one that was injured during a buffalo hunt."

"Where'd you learn to talk their lingo?"

"Not so loud. Learned it from that kid I told you about. I don't want them going on the warpath over this."

"So, what do you suggest?"

"I hate to say this, but you've already tipped your hand. You all but drooled over that horse. Let me handle it."

"Soaring Eagle," Scott said, "Jake wanted to buy that horse for me, but there seems to be something wrong with it."

"What you mean wrong?" Soaring Eagle patted it on the rump. "Good horse. Run fast. Not get tired."

"I can tell just by watching him," Scott said as he placed his hands on his chest and made a motion like his chest expanding. "It doesn't breathe good. What about that gray?"

"Gray not for sale," Soaring Eagle growled.

"What about the Appaloosa?"

"Appaloosa not for sale."

Scott pulled back the canvas that concealed the case of whiskey and said, "I tell you what, Soaring Eagle, that Appaloosa should be taken out and shot, but I'll probably find some idiot to buy it, if it doesn't die on the way back to Whiskey River. So, I'll pitch in the other ten bottles of whiskey for the Appaloosa."

Soaring Eagle conferred with his tribal brothers. After a brief, but heated discussion, Soaring Eagle wheeled and said to Scott, "Nothing wrong with Appaloosa, but I agree just to close deal."

After the Navajos had gathered up all their booty, Jake pulled Scott aside. "How in hell did you pull that off? And what's all this palaver about telling what's wrong with a horse just looking at it?"

"They know the dun is injured. What they don't know is how I figured it out. I suppose they think I have some 'powerful medicine' and if I was right about the dun, I might be right about the Appaloosa too. So my guess is they decided to unload it and take the whiskey and run."

"I wouldn't let on to them you speak their lingo. Might not set too well with them. By the way, I don't see you leaning on that cane anymore. Your ankle must be better."

"I guess Doc Carver was right about staying off it. It really seemed to help."

"Then I reckon you'll be moving on soon."

"I reckon so, unless I can find a good reason to stay."

Chapter Eight

Scott slipped halters on the newly purchased horses and tethered them to the back of the wagon. Jake, impatient to get started, grumbled when Scott ambled over to where Soaring Eagle watched in impassive silence.

"Soaring Eagle. I have a friend. He is one of your people. His name is Bear Heart. I haven't seen him for many years. Do you know him?"

Soaring Eagle nodded. "He is not of this pueblo, but I have heard of him."

"Do you know where I can find him?"

"He worked for the long knives at one time, but not for a good while. It is hard to say where he is."

"It's important that I talk to him. If you hear from him, tell him I have news of his *atsili* from Whiskey River."

"I did not know he had a brother."

*   *   *   *   *

The sun was low in the western sky when Jake and Scott arrived at "La Quebrada del Diablo" an hour away from Whiskey River. The Devil's Pass, more a deep gulch than a gorge, was a long winding narrow stretch. The setting sun cloaked the western wall in shadow spawning a chill on the floor of the pass. There was a hushed calm, the only sounds the muffled plopping of the hooves in the sandy soil. They had made it halfway through the cut when three shots shattered the still air and reverberated up and down the *quebrada*.

Scott, in the lead around a bend, was knocked from his saddle and lay motionless in the sand. The sound of horses retreating from the rim of the gulch broke the ensuing silence.

The wagon team, spooked by the shots, bolted straight ahead, but the horses tethered to the back of the wagon lunged in the opposite direction. This tug of war between the frantic animals turned the wagon on its side leaving Jake pinned underneath.

The pain in Scott's left shoulder, a throbbing, burning sensation, was intense. He lay still while he flexed his fingers, then his wrist, glad to learn that everything worked. He followed the sound of retreating hoof beats and scanned the rim of the pass. Nothing. He lifted himself to a sitting position and winced as a searing pain shot through his arm. He clutched his shoulder and let out a muffled groan. When he pulled his hand away, it was wet with blood that saturated his sleeve. He stared in disbelief at his bloody fingers.

Then he heard Jake calling, "Scott, you there? You all right?"

"Over here, Jake. Took a bullet to the shoulder. Thank God that whoever bushwhacked us would never win a turkey shoot."

"Then get your butt over here and get this wagon off me."

When Scott appeared around the bend, Jake spied the bloody sleeve at the same time Scott saw Jake trapped under the wagon.

"How bad you hit, son?"

"Doesn't seem to be too bad. I can move my arm, but it hurts like hell. How about you?"

"Well, I can wiggle my toes and ankle, so I reckon nothing's broke, but it's cutting off my circulation. See if you can get me out from under here."

"Yep, but first I have to unhitch the team and untie the horses. If I start pushing on this wagon, it might spook them and they could drag you all over the place."

"Well get to it. I can feel my legs starting to go numb."

To save time, Scott cut the traces with his knife. Next he untied the string of horses and tethered them to a shrub. He put his good shoulder to the wagon, but it wouldn't budge.

"This is no good, Jake. I need a pole to use as a lever, but there's nothing but twigs in this cut. Any suggestions?"

Jake's shirt was drenched in sweat in spite of the chill in the air. "Use the wagon tongue, but hurry up for God's sake."

Scott examined the wagon tongue and shook his head. "I have to remove the pin and I don't have the tools to do it with. So we're going to have to figure out something else."

"Well, whatever it is, get to it. I don't know how much longer I can take this."

"OK, I got it. Let me find that spade we brought along and I'll start shoveling the dirt from under you, but first I have to put some rocks under the wagon so it won't settle as I remove the dirt."

After propping up the wagon, which seemed like an eternity to Jake, Scott started digging. Little by little the pressure eased and Jake groaned in delight when his legs started to tingle with pins and needles. With the little strength he had left, Scott laid the shovel aside and tugged on Jake's shoulders until he was clear of the wagon, then he collapsed on the ground next to him.

What seemed like forever was just a few minutes before Jake stretched his legs and nudged Scott with the toe of his boot and said, "I can feel the circulation in my legs now. Fetch my rifle then you ride into town and come back with help."

Scott checked the position of the setting sun. "I'm not leaving you here. It'll be dark in less than an hour and what if a puma or a pack of coyotes comes by and decide to stay for dinner?"

"I'll be all right. I have the rifle."

"Sorry, Jake. One way or another I'm going to get you up on a horse and we're riding out of here together."

By the time Jake was finally able to stand, the sky had turned from orange to purple. He leaned on the overturned wagon for support before taking a few wobbly steps. He clenched his teeth and grimaced in pain, but with each step his gait got steadier. In the waning light Scott rounded up the horses and, with Jake on the paint and Scott riding bareback on the Appaloosa, they rode in silence into Whiskey River, too weary to talk and too numb with pain to even think.

At the railroad tracks they halted and Jake said, "Any thoughts on who bushwhacked us?"

"I got a pretty good notion, but proving it is going to be another thing. They probably got a dozen witnesses who'll say they haven't left town all day."

"Who they?" Jake said.

"Those two dung balls looking to get even, that's who."

Jake took Scott by his good arm. "Look, son, your ankle's good enough to travel and there's no reason for you to stay. That Snake and his sidekick are bad medicine. Hanging around here is only going to get you dead. Just take the Appaloosa and hightail it out of here."

"Like I said yesterday, I'd stay if I found a good reason to. Well, I got three of them now."

In the reflection of the light coming from the Pearly Gate Saloon, Jake could see by the set of Scott's jaw that no amount of arguing was going to change his mind, so he said, "Three, you say. That's two more than I know of."

Scott simply smiled. "You'll find out."

Chapter Nine

Dusk was on the verge of turning into night when Snake and Marv rode toward town at a full gallop only stopping at the railroad tracks to scan the deserted street. The only action was coming from the Pearly Gate Saloon where they dismounted and looped the reins over the hitching rail and casually checked out the street again to make sure no one had seen them enter town.

The usual poker game was in session at one of the tables while a few ranch hands congregated at the bar badgering MacPhearson.

"Hey, Mac, when you going to hire some girls to work here?" a cowpoke named Shorty said.

MacPhearson feigned surprise. "I bring 'em in all the time. Getting 'em to stay is the problem. One look at your ugly faces and they're on the next stage out of here."

"Well, you better do something, I'm so horny the heifers in the corral are starting to look mighty good," Shorty grumbled.

A cowboy at the end of the bar laughed. "Make sure you pick one that's stump broke, Shorty."

As the saloon erupted in laughter, no one noticed Snake and Marv slip through the bat wing doors and ease into chairs at the nearest table, as if they'd been there all the time.

When the laughter subsided, Snake said, "Stick with the heifers, Shorty, they're not nearly as ugly as MacPhearson's pigs."

•　　•　　•　　•　　•

On their way to the livery, Scott spied two horses in front of the Pearly Gate with steam rising from their flanks in the evening chill. "Those two horses been rode hard, Jake. You know everybody's horse in this town. Whose are they?"

"Can't tell for sure in this light, but if I had to guess I'd say they belong to those two rascals, Snake and Marv."

"Well, let's go take a look. Seems to me a hard ride from La Quebrada del Diablo would get a horse all lathered up. Don't you think?"

Jake nodded. "I'd say so."

They tied up their horses at Hardin's place next door and quietly approached the hitching post in front of the saloon. Scott talked soothingly to the horses as he eased the rifle from its holster. He smelled the breech and whispered, "This one's been fired recently. Check the other one."

Jake examined it and nodded. "This one too. Now what?"

"I say we make our case right now while the evidence is fresh. Otherwise, we might as well forget it. You go round back and slip in the door and keep me covered, just in case."

While Jake made his way to the back of the saloon, Scott returned to the Appaloosa and removed Snake's pistol from the saddlebag and shoved it in his waistband. He paused at the threshold, took a deep breath and crashed through the front door. This brought the proceedings to a halt and a foreboding silence came over the room at the sight of Scott Martin, his bloody left arm dangling at his side, pointing a rifle with his good arm at Snake and Marv.

Marv jumped to his feet and edged away from the table, his eyes glued on the Winchester. Snake, an amused grin playing at the corners of his mouth, leaned back in his chair and said, "Well lookie here. Who woulda thought a man could get hurt like that shoveling horse shit?"

Scott met his gaze and said evenly, "About an hour ago somebody took a shot at Jake and me back at the quebrada. Your horses are all lathered up and blowing hard, and your rifle smells like it's been fired recently. So, what do you suppose I'm thinking right now, you yellow-bellied bastard?"

"Who knows what you're thinking. Marv and me been sitting here for quite a spell." Snake looked around the room and added,

"Ain't that right, folks?"

The room fell silent once again. When no one spoke up, Scott continued through thin lips. "I'm saying you're a liar."

Snake took an involuntary breath and his eyes narrowed. "You wouldn't have the guts to say that if I was toting a gun."

Scott lifted Snake's pistol from his waistband with his left hand and tossed it to him. "You got one now and I still say you're a liar."

With all the attention focused on Scott and Snake, no one noticed Marv slowly ease his gun from its holster. In the ominous silence, the click of the hammer being thumbed back echoed throughout the room. The second click was even louder emanating from the rifle Jake held at Marv's back.

Beads of sweat formed on Marv's brow. His mouth worked, but nothing came out. Finally, he released the hammer and returned the gun to its holster.

"Uh unh," Jake said quietly, "dump the bullets on the floor."

As the bullets bounced one by one on the wood floor, Snake shot a glance at Jake and said over his shoulder, "You've minded your business up to now, Jake. You best keep on minding it. This doesn't concern you. It's between me and your stable hand."

"When somebody bushwhacks a feller who works for me and

my wagon falls on top of me, it concerns the hell out of me," Jake said in a steely voice.

Scott pointed with the rifle to the gun in Snake's hand. "You've got your gun now, what's your play?"

Snake glared at Scott and slowly returned the gun to its holster. "That's easy for you to say when you holding a rifle on me."

Scott released the hammer on the Winchester and tossed it to Snake. "I still say you're yellow-bellied liar. What's your excuse now?"

Jake sidled up to Scott with Marv's rifle leveled at Snake's belly button and together they backed toward the front door. Scott's jaw dropped when Jake said, "The fact that we can't prove you and that dimwit partner of yours was the ones who dry gulched us, don't mean nothing. I know it was you just like I know it was you who murdered Jesse Chandler. Just so you know where I stand, you try this again, you better make sure you kill me, or I'll kick your scrawny ass till you own mama won't know you."

Chapter Ten

The scene in the Pearly Gate after Scott and Jake left was like a Daguerreotype, a moment in time captured on tintype. The frozen subjects locked in whatever position they were in when the shutter snapped. Too stunned to move, too frightened to speak. Abruptly, as if responding to a silent command, the subjects came to life. The poker game resumed, MacPhearson continued polishing the glasses, and the cowhands at the bar hoisted their drinks.

Shorty, his sense of self-preservation dulled by all the brave maker he'd tossed down his gullet, broke the silence. "Hey, Snake, was it you who winged that drifter?"

"Me and Marv was here all the time," Snake snapped. "All of you seen us right."

"I ain't speaking for the rest, but I don't recall seeing you until them two busted in here."

Shorty's slurred reply infuriated Snake. "You saying I'm lying?"

Shorty started to say something, but it was pre-empted by a loud belch. He patted his belly and started over. "I ain't saying that, but it sure is a mighty strange coincidence, your horses all lathered up and two shells missing from your rifle."

Snake kicked his chair back, jumped to his feet and snarled at Shorty, "You call me a liar, you better have something to back it up with."

Shorty staggered away from the bar, belched once more and made an awkward attempt to draw his pistol. Snake's gun was in his hand before Shorty's cleared the holster. Snake fanned the hammer with his left hand and three hollow sounding shots rang out. Shorty dropped his pistol and clutched his chest as he crumpled to the floor with his head resting on the brass foot rail, as blood poured out from the back of it.

Snake waved his pistol menacingly at the others. "You all seen that? He drew first."

MacPhearson circled the bar and looked down at Shorty and then at Snake. "Yep, he drew first, but as drunk as he was he couldn't have hit the side of a barn if he was locked up in it."

"How the hell was I supposed to know that?" Snake said.

"You'd damn well know it if you'd been here as long as you say you was," MacPhearson snapped.

"You calling me a liar too?"

Before he could reply, Shorty let out a low moan. "Ooo, shit.

What the hell happened?"

MacPhearson helped him to his feet and propped him against the bar. He ripped open Shorty's shirt, examined his chest, then turned to face Snake with an incredulous look.

"You didn't shoot him . . . he keeled over from the likker and banged his head on the foot-rail."

Snake was equally incredulous. "Whatta ya mean, I didn't shoot him. Of course I shot him. I couldn't miss at that distance."

"Come see for yourself. There ain't a mark on him."

Snake examined the pistol in his hand before taking careful aim at the batwing door no more than ten feet away. He cocked the hammer and gently squeezed off a shot. A .44 slug at that distance would have knocked the door off its hinges. The door didn't budge, as if it were taunting Snake to try again. Which he did, snapping off the remaining two shots in the cylinder.

In his frustration Snake emptied the cylinder to reload. As the spent cartridges hit the floor, instead of empty shells, he saw fully loaded cartridges. So did everyone else. One of the poker players picked one up, examined it closely and said, "I hate to say this, but it looks like there ain't no gunpowder in these bullets. You been shooting duds."

The saloon erupted into raucous laughter. One cowhand made a pistol with his fingers. "Bang, bang you're dead."

"You missed," howled another.

"Dang, my finger must be shooting blanks."

The room rocked with guffaws.

Snake snatched his rifle from the table, worked the lever and fired in the air. The click of the hammer falling on the empty chamber was as deafening as the boisterous laughter. He worked the action again and fired. Again, again and again.

Shorty couldn't contain himself. "He sure made a jackass out of you. First he gives you back your pistol with blanks in it, then he throws down on you with an empty rifle," he cackled.

Snake reloaded his pistol from his gun belt and fired a shot in the air bringing the hoorawing to a sudden halt.

"OK, that's enough of this shit. The fun's over. Y'all git. Unless somebody thinks otherwise now that I have real bullets in my gun."

One by one they started for the door until MacPhearson spoke up. With his double barrel shotgun leveled at Snake he said, "Hold it everybody. This is my saloon and I say who stays and who goes, and I say everybody goes. NOW! The Pearly Gate is closed for the evening."

Snake glowered at MacPhearson who said evenly, "If you're wondering if I'll pull this trigger, there's only one way to find out. You up to it?"

Snake holstered his gun and shrugged. "Hell, Mac, I ain't got no quarrel with you. It's that sonnuva bitch, Scott Martin, I got a score to settle with."

Chapter Eleven

At the livery, Jake and Scott turned the horses loose in the small corral at the rear. "We'll take care of them in the morning." Jake grumbled. "Right now we better go to the house and take a look at that arm."

"You go ahead. I saw a light on at Doc Carver's place. I think I'll let him take a gander at it after I clean up a bit."

"Maybe I better go with you. That's the second time you showed up that pair of rascals, and they just might be lying in the weeds waiting for you."

"I ain't worried," Scott said with a sly grin, "what Snake doesn't know is that his gun is loaded with blanks."

In reply to Jake's surprised look, Scott said, "The first night on the trail when you were sleeping, I pried the lead out from the bullets, dumped the gun powder out, and tapped the slug back in place. When he shoots that gun, the percussion cap will go off, but won't nothing come out the barrel but a loud bang."

Jake continued to stare incredulously and Scott added, "You don't think I'm that dumb to give him back his gun and goad him into a fight, do you?"

"But you still had the rifle."

Scott held out a handful of .44-40 cartridges. "While you went around the back of the saloon, I ejected all the cartridges, eight of them. That's a short barrel Winchester and it only holds ten cartridges. If he started out with a full magazine, it means he fired two shots and Marv one."

Jake's jaw dropped. "You mean there were no bullets in that rifle?"

A devilish grin played at the corners of Scott's mouth. "I'd sure like to see Snake's face when he discovers I had him covered with an empty rifle."

They broke out in uncontrollable laughter and all the tension of the previous two hours drained from them like water through a busted dam. When they stopped to catch their breath, Scott said, "Guess I'll clean up 'fore I mosey over to Doc Carver's. If nothing else I know I can count on him for a dose or two of his favorite painkiller."

•　　•　　•　　•　　•

Once in his room Scott removed his shirt and examined his left shoulder in the mirror above the washstand. In the yellow light of the kerosene lantern the blood encrusted wound looked grisly. Just as he lifted the porcelain pitcher to fill the basin with water, there was a knock on the door. Before he could reply, Laura walked in carrying an armload of towels, various medicinals, and bandages. Without a word she deposited the first aid supplies on the bed and stood, hands on her waist admiring Scott's bare torso that tapered to narrow hips. Although she was no stranger to blood and gore, an involuntary gasp escaped from her throat when her gaze shifted to his shoulder.

She quickly regained her composure and said, "So you went and got yourself all shot up. Is that all you men know how to do?" Her tone belied the inexplicable emotions that swirled inside her. "Let me take a look at that."

With no father around since he was six years old, Scott learned to trust his instincts and fend for himself. Independent and self-reliant, he took his time warming up to people, and because of that they saw him as a loner. Scott fancied himself more like a hound dog that, when hurt, just wanted to crawl under the porch and lie down until he got better. He didn't want to be trifled with. His annoyance was short lived, however, until Laura in a bright yellow shirtwaist tucked into snug denim pants, left him groping for a reply.

"I thought I'd go see Doc Carver and let him take a gander at it," Scott mumbled.

"You're just as well off with me, maybe even better since he's probably passed out by now. Besides I'm sort of his nurse."

"How'd you come by that job?"

"At first it was just to drive the buggy, to keep him from getting lost, but more and more he let me do things a nurse would do. His hands aren't as steady as they used to be, so once we got where we were going, he showed me what needed to be done."

"Like what?"

"At first it was just patching up banged up cowboys and dressing wounds. Before you know it I was delivering babies, digging out bullets and setting broken bones."

"Well, in that case what are we waiting for, Nurse Laura? Let's get on with it."

"We can start by cleaning up this mess if you'll stop your jabbering and stand still."

She held his arm firmly in her left hand and with the other she washed away the dried blood with alcohol. The firmness and warmth of his triceps against her hand sent messages to her brain that made it difficult to concentrate on what she was doing. Her heart was aflutter and her hand wasn't as steady as it usually is.

Get a grip on yourself, woman.

Her soft touch, the fragrant scent of her hair, and the nearness of her body stirred up feelings in Scott too powerful to ignore. His arousal, not unnoticed by Laura, was short-lived, however. The searing pain of the antiseptic she dabbed on the wound brought an abrupt end to his erotic notions.

Laura clucked at him. "Tell me something, Mr. Martin. Do you find pain sexually stimulating?"

Scott reddened but couldn't help grinning in spite of himself. "I reckon it's got more to do with you than the pain."

It was Laura's turn to blush. "You're a lucky man. The bullet went clean through, missed the bone and didn't appear to have hit any nerves or major blood vessels. You should be as good as new. Of course that's only my inexpert opinion. You may want to see Doc Carver to confirm it."

"I'll take your word for it. I reckon the only thing Doc would do different is hand me three fingers of pain killer in a dirty glass."

"I can go one better. I'll serve it in a clean glass. Come over to the house and I'll see what's left of supper."

Laura turned to gather her supplies, but Scott took her arm and pulled her toward him. "I must owe you something for this. Whatever Doc charges, I'll pay double."

Laura tried to avoid his eyes lest he see the desire smoldering behind her own, but she couldn't take her eyes off him. Deep within her spirit Laura wondered if she had finally met the man she wanted to settle down with, but how could she? He was nothing but a drifter, a "tumbleweed" he had said, and she didn't want to be just another of his adventures before he moved on to the next one.

She pushed away and said with a laugh, "What are you going to pay me with, if you didn't even have train fare?"

"How about I work it off. I'm sure there's something you'd like me to do for you."

Laura assumed a thoughtful pose. "Come to think about it, there is. Since you're so good at dishing out that crap, you can spread the manure on the vegetable garden."

Chapter Twelve

Jake was just finishing dinner when Laura and Scott walked in. Teresa got up to remove the serving dishes from the oven and motioned for them to sit.

"Don't know how good this'll be, setting in the oven that long," she grumbled.

"After four days of Jake's cooking, prairie dogs would be a treat," Scott replied.

Teresa sniffed, "Humph."

"I apologize for letting the food get cold. I know how you hate that, but Laura insisted on patching me up first. Blame it on her."

Teresa's demeanor softened. "Apology accepted. By the way, Laura, how bad is his arm?"

"Just a flesh wound. He'll live, but his arm will be sore for a few days."

After serving herself a second helping of lamb stew Teresa said, "You sure have muddied up the waters since you got here. You made fools out of those two tinhorn gunslingers, got Sam

Hardin all riled up, and almost got yourself killed today. Whatever you're here for, I sure hope it's worth it."

Scott ate in silence while pondering his response, but Jake pushed his plate away, leaned back in his chair and said, "What I can't figure out is if those two varmints are just trying to get even, or if they're acting on Hardin's orders."

"Why would Sam Hardin be behind this? What has Scott done to him?" Laura asked quietly.

"That's just the point. Maybe Hardin knows something we don't," Jake said and shot a meaningful look at Scott.

Scott felt Jake's eyes burning into his head. He put down his knife and fork and spoke slowly. "I'm just as much in the dark as you are. From the moment I got tossed off the train, the only ones who stuck out a friendly hand are you folks. Seems like everybody else either wants me gone or wants me dead. The inhospitable part I can deal with, but I take it real personal when somebody's out to kill me. I'm a curious sort and I decided to stick around to find out why. I'm really sorry I dragged Jake into it. If it'll help any, I'll find some place else to stay."

"There ain't no other place where you can stay, without money that is," Jake said. "Besides, you didn't drag me into nothing. I know what I'm doing."

"Funny you should say that, Jake, because I wanted to ask you about what you said in the saloon. You know, about you accusing Snake of murdering Jesse Chandler."

Laura and Teresa exchanged quick glances.

"I thought we agreed we'd never bring that up," Teresa snapped.

"We did, but ever since the day Scott got here, something's been gnawing at me to set things right. Like his arriving here was a sign. Don't know exactly what it is, but I just know it's right."

Scott's eyes went from Jake to Teresa to Laura and back to Jake. "Never bring what up?"

"Sam Hardin paid Snake Weston to kill Jesse Chandler. Told him to set it up so it would look all legal like."

"Can you prove that?"

"That's just the point . . . I can't prove it . . . I just know what I know."

"That's a pretty strong accusation without any proof," Scott said.

"All I know is this. Right after the shooting I was in one of the stables looking after a colicky horse when Snake Weston and Sam Hardin met at the back of the livery. Hardin handed Weston a pouch and said, 'That was real slick. Yes, sir, real slick. Here's your five hundred dollars. Now you and your idiot sidekick get the hell out of Whiskey River' and he started to walk away, but . . ."

"But what," Scott said, his eyes boring into Jake's.

"Snake kinda laughed and said, 'I don't figger on getting the hell out of no place. I sorta like it here. Besides, that five hundred is just a down payment. Marv and me are now officially on your payroll. You know, to make sure nobody else gets any funny notions about who's running this place.' "

"How did Hardin take that?"

"He was flabbergasted. He ain't used to people telling him what to do. He yelled at them, threatened them, but must have realized they had him by the short and curlies. All of a sudden he calms down and says they'd talk about it."

"And you never did anything about it," Scott remarked, more of a statement than a question.

"What the hell could I do? The nearest law was in Santa Fe, a two days ride, and it was my word against his. Beside, Marv would swear that Chandler went for the Derringer that was in his waistband."

"The one Marv planted on him," Scott said.

"Exactly."

"Whatever happened to that gun?" Scott asked.

"Come to think about it, I don't rightly know. At first there was a lot of commotion, then Doc shows up. Pretty soon Jesse is sitting up and before you know it, he gets up and staggers out the place. Next thing we know he's on his horse hightailing it out of town."

Teresa rose and stood behind Jake. "You don't know how much this has troubled Jake. We wrote Sarah, his wife, but she never answered. We figured she just wanted to be shed of the whole affair. Besides, it was over two years since she left and, not hearing anything back from her, we reckoned she just wanted to close the book on that part of her life."

Scott shook his head slowly. "It's hard for me to believe his wife would ignore something like that."

Jake loaded his pipe and dropped a casual remark as he tamped the tobacco. "What makes you say that? What do you know about her?"

"Only from what you've told me," Scott said with a bland expression. "She just doesn't seem like the kind of person who would run away from a fight."

"That she isn't," Teresa said, "at least when we knew her she wasn't and that's why it surprised us when we didn't hear from her. It was like she didn't even get the letter."

Scott nodded thoughtfully. "Now there's an idea, but that

doesn't get us any closer to proving Hardin put Snake up to it."

"Wait a minute, son, this ain't none of your affair. You just mind your own business and let us handle this."

Scott pushed away from the table and got to his feet. "Well, I'm making it my affair."

Touching the bandage on his arm he went on, "I believe I've bought into this pot and you damn well know that varmint, Snake, isn't going to let your accusation go unchallenged. From now on I'm watching your back and you're watching mine until this hand is played out."

· · · · ·

Laura followed Scott to the front porch and closed the door behind her. "Scott, be careful. Sam Hardin is a ruthless man. Believe me, I know. Maybe you should take Jake's advice and just go wherever it is you're going."

"That's just the point, I don't have any place to go. Besides who's going to patch me up when I get banged around?"

Laura looked away, a profusion of thoughts muddling her brain. *If he knows what's good for him he really should hightail it out of here. At the same time I'm glad he's staying. He stirs up feelings in me like no man has ever done before. But what good can come of falling for a saddle tramp? Yet, he doesn't seem to be an ordinary drifter. Stop it! Get those notions out of your head.*

Laura turned to face Scott. "That's just the problem, Scott. I guess I'd like you to stay, but not if it's going to get you hurt."

Scott winced as he lifted his hands to Laura's face. "I'll be real careful." He tilted her face up and kissed her. He felt her arms encircle his neck as she kissed him back.

Just as abruptly she pushed away and let out a deep breath. "My word, Mr. Martin, it's obvious pain isn't the only thing that arouses you."

Scott grinned. "I believe I'll mention that to Doc Carver when I see him in the morning and see if he can fix it."

"I'd think that over very carefully if I were you," Laura shot back over her shoulder as she headed for the door.

Chapter Thirteen

More than the throbbing pain in his arm, something bothered Scott more. He couldn't stop thinking about the way Laura kissed him the previous night. He'd never been kissed like that before . . . a hungry passionate kiss. He struggled into his pants and grimaced as he eased his injured arm into the sleeve of his shirt, which turned out to be the easy part. Fastening the buttons with one hand was more of a challenge.

He had just tucked the tail of his shirt into his britches when Laura pushed her way unannounced into his room, carrying a pot of coffee and a plate full of biscuits and jelly.

"Good morning. I don't expect the sick and the wounded to make it for breakfast, so I thought I'd bring you something to eat. I see you're already dressed. What a pity, you've deprived me of the opportunity to demonstrate some of my other nursing skills."

Scott felt his ears turning red. *What is it about this woman that can make me blush like a schoolboy?*

"My, am I embarrassing you?"

"Well, you . . . you certainly know how to make man uneasy," Scott stammered.

Laura, hands on her hips clucked her tongue. "Look at you, you can't even button your shirt right."

With nimble fingers she deftly unbuttoned his shirt and refastened the buttons correctly. Scott could feel the blood rising to his cheeks again. "Miss Randle," he said, "you're going to have to stop being so forward. I mean, a proper woman would knock before entering a man's bedroom. What will people think?"

"Mr. Scott Martin, I've always done pretty much as I please, and what people think is of no concern to me."

"Just the same, it makes me feel kind of awkward, and about last night, I apologize for taking such liberties."

Laura tilted her head to one side and said, "You didn't take anything I wasn't willing to give. Now, eat your breakfast before it gets cold."

•　　•　　•　　•　　•

It was around eight o'clock when Scott stepped out of the livery and headed for Doc Carver's place. He was abreast of the undertaker's place when a voice called out to him, "Can you spare a minute? I'd like to have a word with you."

Scott looked across the street and saw Sam Hardin standing in the open doorway of his office. He studied Hardin for a moment before casting a glance up and down the street.

"Don't worry. There's nobody else here. Just you and me. Come on over."

Scott crossed the street and went through the door Hardin held open for him. Hardin took a seat at his desk and invited Scott to sit in a chair facing him.

"I believe in getting right down to business," Hardin said before continuing, "I'd like to know if you'd be interested in a proposition."

"Go ahead. I'm listening."

"I've just about had my fill of those two hotheads who work for me and their shenanigans. They haven't got the sense God gave a jackass. They take off on their own causing all kinds of trouble, and I've run out of patience with them."

"Why should that concern me?" Scott asked.

"Look here. I ain't saying they're the ones who took pot shots at you, but then again, I wouldn't put it past them. Seeing as how they work for me, folks might get the wrong idea . . . like I'm the one behind it, which I'm not. That's the kind of trouble I'm talking about."

"So, what's your proposition?"

Hardin leaned back in his swivel chair and bridged his fingers. "I can't imagine you getting rich forking hay in the livery, so I'd like to give you a chance to make some money and get out of here."

Scott cocked his head to one side and said, "I'm always interested in making a buck."

"Okay, here's the deal. Those two idiots . . . well, I gotta get rid of them. They're too much of a liability . . . too unpredictable."

"So, why don't you just fire them? Give 'em a couple month's pay and tell them to skedaddle."

"The problem with that is, they been working for me so long, they might not want to leave peaceable like, unless I give them a lot more encouragement."

"And you want me to encourage them to pursue other interests, preferably somewhere else."

"Well, I would put it a little stronger. I'd feel a lot better if something happened to them so they never pursued anything ever again."

Scott came forward in his chair. "I see. So let's get to the nut-cutting. What's in it for me to deprive these two upstanding citizens of life, liberty, and the pursuit of happiness?"

"Five hundred dollars and you clear out once it's over."

Scott leaned back in the chair. "How do I know you're not

setting me up?"

"Why in the world would I do that? I have nothing against you."

"Well, five days ago you wanted me out of here and the next day your weasels jumped me in the saloon. Let's not kid ourselves, they're the ones who bushwhacked me in the quebrada."

"Look, that ambush was all their idea," Hardin argued. "You made jackasses out of them and that's the only way they know how to settle anything."

"Just the same," Scott replied, "it seems like a no lose proposition for you. You win if I get rid of them, and you win if I die trying, except in that case you'd still be stuck with them."

"I'm betting on you. You look like you can take care of yourself. What's more, you're a hell of a lot smarter and you ain't afraid of them."

"How do I know you're not making the same deal with Snake? Like you did once before."

"If you're insinuating I put them up to that incident in Devil's Pass, you're wrong."

"Mr. Hardin, that isn't what I'm referring to."

Hardin glowered at Scott. "I have no idea what you're talking about."

"Jake Morgan feels like you put Snake up to killing that Jesse Chandler."

"I had nothing to do with that. Chandler was a drunk who got caught cheating and got himself killed in a shoot-out," Hardin said hotly.

It seemed to Scott that Hardin was protesting a mite too much. He stood and marched toward the door. With his hand on the knob he said, "Let me think about it."

●   ●   ●   ●   ●

Scott stood outside Hardin's office trying to appear calm, but his knees were weak and his hands shook as the tension poured out of his body. When he had calmed down sufficiently to walk steadily, he put on his hat and strode toward Doc Carver's house. On the way his musings took him to what Laura had said about Hardin. *She's right, that is one dangerous man. If I had any doubts about his masterminding Jesse Chandler's death, he just dispelled them. He doesn't get his hands dirty . . . he let's someone else do his dirty work.*

Doc's door was ajar so Scott invited himself in. The place was the same as the first day he was there . . . like a cyclone had hit it then came back to finish what it missed the first time. A gravel voice called out from the rear, "Have a seat. Be right out to take a look at that arm."

"How the hell you knew it was me?"

Doc Carver appeared slipping his suspenders over his shoulders and looking surprisingly alert. "Heard all about it from Shorty. Somebody dumped him at my front door where I found him this morning. He had a hell of a gash on the back of his head. So, let's take a look at that arm."

Scott unbuttoned his shirt and slipped his left arm out of the sleeve. "Laura Randle patched me up last night."

Doc undid Laura's bandage and said, "That's one helluva woman. Damn sight better than a lot of the real nurses I worked with back in St. Louis. Wish I'd met her when I was younger."

Doc poked and probed and debrided some of the dead tissue, then doused the wound with an antiseptic before putting a new bandage on it. He handed Scott a bottle of whiskey and said, "This is for the pain if you need it."

Scott groaned and waved it away. Doc took the bottle, poured himself three fingers in a glass he wiped clean with his bandanna, and leaned back in his chair. "Young feller, I told you the first time I saw you that if you hung around here you'd end up in a pine box. Now, tell me just what is it that makes you so hard-headed."

Scott eyed Doc, sizing him up carefully. "Can we talk confidentially, doctor-patient like? As one professional to another?"

"I don't know what you mean professional, but as far as confidentiality, I ain't talked to nobody about nothing for years. Don't see any reason to start now."

Scott nodded, then began to speak. "I'm a lawyer, but I haven't practiced any law. You see, I just graduated and I'm working on my first case. Been hired by a client to prove that someone has wrongfully appropriated property that belonged to my client's family. My client's family received the property under a Spanish land grant, and when New Mexico became a territory of the United States, the land grant was recognized as valid. My client still holds the deed to the property."

"So what the hell you doing here? All those records are in Santa Fe."

"I know," Scott agreed, "but first I wanted to get a feel for the situation without people knowing what I was up to. I wanted to see what I was up against."

Doc knocked back half the whiskey in his glass and said, "I take it that piece of property is right here in Whiskey River, and if I ain't mistaken, it's what Sam Hardin claims is his. Right?"

Scott responded with a wry smile.

"And," Doc continued, "your client is Sarah Chandler."

Scott nodded. "Right again."

"Why, after all these years, would she be stirring up those old ashes?"

Scott shrugged. "She didn't confide her reasons with me. Maybe you can answer that question better than me. You knew her, and her husband, Jesse, as well, right?"

"Knew her better than most folks here."

"What can you tell me about her . . . I mean without betraying a confidence?"

Doc drained the rest of the whisky and poured himself a replacement. "There was a lot going on back then. Some of it I can talk about, some I can't. But this much I can say, Sarah never would have left here on her own. Something or somebody drove her away. Whatever it was must have been real painful for her to pack up and leave like that and never come back."

Scott motioned to a glass on the desk and said, "It's a little early for me, but I think I'll have a wee one."

He tossed half of it back and shuddered. "I'm curious, Doc. I hear you're one helluva doctor. What the heck are you doing in Whiskey River?"

Doc Carver stared out the side window, the one facing the train tracks and drummed his fingers on the desk. When he stopped the drumming, the hand started to shake imperceptibly. He turned back to Scott and said, "At some point in everyone's life they have a choice to make . . . face their demons or run away from them. I, like Sarah, chose not to face them."

"And what are your demons, Doc?" Scott said in a quiet voice.

"You're an educated man. I could see that right off the first day you came in here."

Scott winked at Doc.

Doc went on, "Ever hear of Ambroise Pare?"

"Can't say as I have."

"He was a French surgeon who lived in the 1500's. He discovered one of the main causes of impotence in men, but a lot of people thought he was a quack, as well as anyone who accepted his theory. Medically the problem is what's called a variocele that blocks blood supply to the penis preventing an erection."

"What's that got to do with you?"

Doc raised his hand to quiet Scott. "By the time I became a surgeon it was widely accepted, and I became the local expert on the subject, as well as sterility in both men and women, but there were still some doctors, especially in St. Louis, who were skeptical. Well, I had a patient, one of the most influential men in town, whose ego was as big as the Mississippi River. He was also impotent but you wouldn't know it from the amount of time he spent in the city's pleasure parlors, in spite of having a charmingly beautiful wife. Stories abounded among the 'ladies of the evening' that he couldn't "perform," and how he paid them to extol his sexual prowess."

"I still don't get the point," Scott said.

"The point is, his wife got tired of hearing all the gossip about her impotent husband's escapades, so she comes to me and asks if I could do something because she wanted children. I told her if she wanted children, she better think about adoption or getting someone other than her husband to do the job."

Scott nodded. "I see. Let me guess, she didn't like the idea of adopting and you became the someone other than her husband."

"You got that one figured right."

"Something tells me it was more than a service you were providing. You loved her didn't you?"

Doc nodded and stared out the window again and was silent for a long time.

"You want to tell me the rest of it?" Scott asked gently.

Doc sighed and continued, "When she turned up pregnant, he went into a rage and killed her. Not only killed her, but our child as well."

"Oh, my God. What a beast."

"That sonnuva bitch came to see me, because he knew I was seeing her, as her doctor, not as her lover, and he asked me if I knew who the father was. I was only too happy to tell him . . . right before I beat him senseless . . . the way he beat his wife. Then I emasculated him. I dragged the bastard to my laboratory and closed up the office . . . told everybody I had a family emergency back East. By the time they found the body I was here in Whiskey River."

While Doc stared into his glass of mind numbing liquor, Scott studied the walls of the room. Absent were the usual diplomas or certificates, which prompted him to ask, "Has your name always been Carver?"

Doc allowed himself a malevolent grin.

"No, I thought Carver would be an appropriate alias."

Scott raised his glass to Doc Carver. " I agree to be your lawyer and in exchange for my *pro bono* legal services you agree to provide free medical service and advice. Under such an arrangement, lawyer-client and doctor-patient to wit, we are obliged to observe whatever transpires between us as privileged information."

Doc lifted his glass in acknowledgment. "I'll drink to that . . .

or anything else that occurs to you."

"As a matter of fact, one other thing does occur to me. What prompted Abigail Randle to ask Teresa Morgan to take Laura in case of her demise?"

"Young man, that also is privileged information, but it's not between you and me. And, I'll thank you to leave now."

Chapter Fourteen

Jake snatched a horseshoe from the forge with his tongs and placed it on the anvil. Sweat rolled down his arms and his bulging biceps glistened as he lifted the heavy mall to form a shoe for one of the new ponies. While the shoe lay cooling Scott returned from his visit with Doc Carver.

Jake wiped the sweat from his face with his bandanna and said, "Did Doc say you're fit enough to do some real work around here?"

Scott shrugged in mock apology. "Nothing but light work and no heavy lifting."

"Well, we got to shoe all the new ponies. If leading a horse by the halter qualifies as light work, you can start by bringing out the mare."

Jake exchanged his hammer for the dipper hanging on a nail and drew himself a drink from the water bucket. Over the rim of the dipper he observed a rider on a chestnut Appaloosa approaching the north end of town. At the tracks the rider reined in his horse to study the layout of the town.

Jake shaded his eyes with his hat and noticed that an Indian blanket was the only thing that separated the rider from the horse. He appeared to be Indian, but his only concession to native dress was his moccasins and the colorful headband that held back the long black hair that fell to his shoulders. The stranger scanned the street once again, then urged his mount forward across the tracks and headed for the livery. He got as far as the Pearly Gate when Snake Weston and his buddy, Marv, stepped off the verandah and took positions in the street to block his way.

"Where the hell you think you going, Injun?" Snake snarled.

The stranger reined in the horse, his expressionless face belying the anger seething within.

"I have business here," the Indian replied in an even tone.

"You talk pretty good English for a redskin. What kind of business?"

"That is none of your affair, now please get out of my way," the Indian said quietly.

"I aim to make it my business, Injun, and you ain't going nowhere 'til you tell me what you doing here."

Scott emerged from the stable leading the mare and joined Jake at the water bucket where they both took in the scene unfolding in front of the saloon. All of a sudden he handed the rope to Jake and dashed to his room. He reappeared seconds later carrying his rifle and strode silently toward the saloon.

As he got closer, he could hear Snake taunting the Indian. "You know, you don't look like no Injun to me. You some kind of half-breed? Must have been your daddy who was the white one. No white woman would let an Injun touch her. Ain't that right, Marv?"

Marv cackled like the idiot he was. "Right as rain, Snake."

The Indian touched his heels to the horse's flanks, but before the horse could take two steps, Snake and Marv both drew their pistols and fired several shots at its feet. The horse reared and side stepped several times before spinning out of control. The Indian found himself on his back still hanging on to the reins.

"You know what's good for you Injun, you'll get right back on that horse and ride out of town. But, before you do that you're going to a little dance for us. You Injuns are supposed to be good at dancing. Ain't that right?"

The Indian got to his feet and puffs of dust rose as Marv fired at his feet. The Indian stood his ground and glared at his tormentors before fixing his eyes on an object behind them. Snake spun around to see what caught the Indian's attention and found himself staring down the barrel of Scott's rifle.

Snake sucked in a deep breath and took an involuntary step backward. He quickly recovered from the shock and growled. "Stay out of this stable boy. This ain't none of your affair."

Scott's steel gray eyes smoldered with rage. "And it ain't none of your affair what this man is doing here."

"We don't allow Injuns, and that includes half-breeds, in town. I'm just enforcing the rule."

"There's only one rule you got to follow, you yellow-bellied offspring of a border town whore, and this is it. This man is my friend. You trifle with him again, and you got me to deal with. Now shove those guns back in their holsters and get the hell out of his way."

Snake and Marv glowered at Scott and reluctantly holstered their guns.

"We ain't done with you yet, stable boy."

"Turn around and start walking and don't stop until you're off the street."

By this time, alerted by the gunshots, the entire boardwalk, from the dressmaker's shop to the Emporium, was lined with people. Children in the one room schoolhouse poured out of the windows like it was on fire to join them. They all watched in awe as Snake and Marv slunk off to the saloon, like the curs they were.

"That feller's buying himself a heap of trouble," someone murmured.

"If he knows what's good for him, he'll get out of town while he' still drawing breath," another said.

"I dunno, looks like Snake and Marv are the ones who ought to be thinking of clearing out. That young feller sure is a burr under their saddle."

Sam Hardin stood in the doorway of his office scratching his chin and wondering if maybe he was a bit hasty in offering Scott Martin five hundred dollars to get rid of those two jackasses. He figured that if he left them alone long enough, they'd do themselves in on their own.

The crowd slowly dispersed when Scott and the Indian took off in the direction of the livery.

* * * * *

"Jake, this is my friend, Billy Bear Heart."

Billy took Jakes's outstretched hand and said, "I've heard of you and what a sharp horse trader you are."

"A man's got to be sharp when dealing with Soaring Eagle. Right glad to meet you, Billy. Scott mentioned you and him knew each other when you were kids."

"We went to the same school."

"If it's any of my business, how did you end up in the same school?" Jake asked.

"My father was a white man, and my mother made me go to school to learn the white man's ways."

"And where was that?"

"In Las Cruces," Billy said without hesitation.

Jake glanced at Scott. "You never mentioned anything about Las Cruces."

Scott shrugged. "We moved around a lot. Been lots of places."

"So what brings you to Whiskey River, Billy?"

"I got word from Soaring Eagle that Scott was here and wanted to see me."

"I see. Well, I guess you two got a lot of catching up to do. See ya later."

•　　•　　•　　•　　•

Once inside Scott's room they embraced, then laughed like they did when they were kids.

"Las Cruces? How the hell you come up with that?"

Billy shrugged. "It's a good a place as any, but how come

you're not Luke any more?"

"I'll tell you in a minute, but what have you been doing all this time?"

Billy shrugged. "Not much. I was an interpreter for the government while the tribe was in Bosque Redondo. But they've all gone back to their lands and I live outside of Santa Fe. I still get some jobs from the Government. How about you?"

"Believe it or not, I managed to finish law school, and I am now a lawyer."

"You a lawyer? If it weren't for me you would have rotted in fifth grade. So what the hell you doing here in Whiskey River?"

"Seeing how I can help get Mrs. Chandler's property back."

Billy's eyebrows shot up. "I can't believe it. So, she's finally decided to do something about it. I wonder what made her change her mind."

"I wouldn't go so far as to say she's changed her mind. In fact, she doesn't even know I'm here. This is something I've got to do on my own."

Billy nodded his head in approval. "I guess if I was in your shoes, I'd feel the same way, but, what the hell, whatever the reason, I'm glad. I always liked and respected her. She was the best teacher I ever had."

Scott shot him a sidelong glance and said, "I thought you went to school in Las Cruces."

Chapter Fifteen

Scott buckled the strap on his rucksack and said, "So now you see, Billy, why I came here incognito . . . to try to get a handle on what legal avenues are open to me. If I can get Jake to testify at a trial about what he heard, I think I can get Hardin on conspiracy to commit murder and put a noose around the neck of those two yahoos, Snake and Marv."

"What trial?" Billy scoffed. "There ain't even a sheriff here, much less a judge."

"That's why I have to go to Santa Fe. I need to talk to the U.S. Marshal and swear out a complaint. That way a judge will have to hear the case. If that won't work, I'll just have to figure out another way to bring him to justice."

"Why waste your time?" Billy said. "There's only one kind of justice out here."

"But, what if Jake is wrong? What if Jesse Chandler did owe him all that money? What if Jesse did draw first?"

"It still didn't give him the right to just grab the land and screw

Sarah Chandler out of what's rightfully hers, Scott."

"I know, Billy, but I've got to be sure. I believe in a different kind of justice. Just because you can draw a gun faster and shoot straighter than the other guy doesn't make it fair."

"It sure in hell worked for the Army," his voice turning bitter. "They drove my people off their lands and corralled them like animals at Bosque Redondo. Where's the justice in that?"

"What's this Bosque Redondo, Billy? That's the second time you've brought it up."

"It's a large grove of cottonwoods up on the Pecos. The Army rounded up eight thousand of my people in Arizona and drove 'em like cattle for three hundred miles. The 'Long March" they call it. Once they got there they kept them penned up like goats for four years before they let them return. The Army called it a reservation, but it was more like a prison camp. Like I said, where's the justice in that?"

Scott heaved a deep sigh and put his arm around Billy's shoulders. "That's exactly what I'm talking about, Billy. There is no justice in that, and I don't want to be guilty of anything even close to that."

•　　•　　•　　•　　•

Two more strokes to trim the hoof and Jake was finished with the mare. He laid the rasp on the anvil and, with both hands on his hips, arched his back to relieve his tired muscles. The sun was almost overhead and dust devils, raised by the breeze whistling through the town, did pirouettes in the deserted street. A stray dog loped across the street, flies buzzed over clumps of horse apples, and buzzards circled effortlessly in the sky . . . the only creatures daring to brave the scorching, midday sun.

Jake dipped a drink from the water bucket and studied Scott and Billy as they approached. He tossed out the remnants in the dipper and wiped his mouth on his sleeve. "What have you two been up to? From that sly look on your faces, I'd say you two have something up your sleeve."

"Nah, nothing mysterious. Billy's heading back to Santa Fe and I've decided to go with him. On the way we'll go by Devil's Pass and set the wagon on its wheels so you can fetch it with the team. I'll be back in about a week. Mind if I take the Appaloosa?"

Jake studied the two of them closely. "Any particular reason you're going to Santa Fe?"

Scott shrugged. "Nothing special. I always heard a lot about it and thought I'd go see for myself. Besides it'll give Billy and me a chance to catch up on old times."

Jake squinted at Scott. "It takes money to hang around a place like Santa Fe, money you ain't got."

"That's not a problem. Billy has some from when he was working for the Army."

Jake looked up at the sun. "Getting on about noon time. Why don't we mosey up to the house and after lunch Teresa can pack some vittles for you."

On the side of the house there was a washstand where Laura was scrubbing dirt from the vegetables freshly harvested from the garden. Wisps of her dark hair fell in disarray from under her wide-brim straw hat and tiny beads of sweat trickled down her cheeks. The bright colors of the tomatoes, squashes, carrots, and peppers were no match for her radiant glow. She gave Scott and Billy a casual glance as they approached and brushed a stray tendril with the back of her hand.

"So, what did Doc Carver think of my patchwork?"

"He said you keep it up and he's out of a job."

"Sure he did," she said as she wiped both sides of her hands on the seat of her pants and thrust one forward to Billy. "Who's your friend?"

"This is Billy Bear Heart. We went to school together over seven years ago."

"Billy, I'm Laura. I'm not so sure the folks in Whiskey River will take kindly to you being here, but you're welcome here anytime."

Billy took her hand. "You have a firm grip. Shows strong character. A lot of men are afraid of women like that. Thank you for the welcome."

Laura gave Billy a "who you trying to kid" look and smiled at his gallantry. "Now I see where Scott gets his palaver from, or is it the other way around?"

Scott felt his ears grow hot, but before he could defend himself, Jake intervened. "These two are taking off for Santa Fe after lunch."

Laura eyes fell, an act not lost on Jake, who quickly added, "But Scott says he'll be back in a week."

Laura's look was skeptical. "That right, Scott?"

Scott nodded. "Sure I will, too much unfinished business here to tend to."

Laura attempted a smile all the while wondering if she was part of the unfinished business. "Well, what are we standing around for? Y'all get washed up and Teresa and I well get lunch on the table."

. . . . .

At their customary table in the Pearly Gate, Snake was in a

black mood and Marv was doing his best to humor him. "Hell, Snake, it ain't like he outdrew you. I mean sneaking up on a feller from behind don't count as a gunfight. What else could you do when he's got the drop on you? I seen you outdraw lots of men, and this jasper wouldn't stand a chance with you. No, siree, he'd be dead 'fore his gun cleared the holster, that is, if he had the guts to carry one."

Snake poured out three fingers of whiskey and scowled at the glass. "You're right. He's a yellow bellied coward who won't stand up to a fight. So we just got to corner the sonnuva bitch 'til he's got no choice. Jest gotta figure out a way to do it."

•　　•　　•　　•　　•

Scott and Billy led their horses out of the livery ready to mount up for their trek to Santa Fe. They found Laura waiting with a bundle wrapped in a heavy cloth. "Don't dilly dally on the way, there's only enough food for a couple of days. Don't know what you're going to do for the way back."

"Oh, I'm sure he can find a *señorita* or two in Santa Fe to take care of that," Billy teased. What happened so quickly no one saw it coming, a left hook that left Scott rubbing his jaw. Laura, in semi-shock, threw the food at Billy and ran toward the house.

Jake removed his pipe from the bib of his overalls and said, "You know what, Scott? I think she really likes you."

"If that's the way she shows how she likes someone, I sure don't want to get on her bad side," Scott observed massaging his jaw.

Jake filled the bowl of the pipe and nodded gravely, "I wouldn't recommend that either."

At the rear of the livery Scott saddled the Appaloosa, jet black with characteristic white markings, and placed the grub in one of the saddlebags. In the other one he stowed his money belt along with his pistol and gun belt. Billy arranged the blanket on his horse, grabbed the mane in is left hand and in one easy motion was aboard his mount.

After Scott mounted his horse he said, "Billy, I think it's best if we circle our way out of town. We don't have time to trifle with two bung holes again"

"Suits me. Let's ride."

•   •   •   •   •

Jake had just led the second horse to be shoed out of the stable when three short blasts and two long ones from the train's whistle shattered the early after silence. He tethered the animal and made his way to the edge of the tracks to join the crowd, who like Jake, were perplexed that the train was gracing Whiskey River with another visit for the second time in less than a week. Likewise, the patrons of the Pearly Gate Saloon, who stood on the verandah with their drinks still in their hands. Likewise, Doc Carver who remained in the shade of his porch with his ever-present glass of whiskey. In fact, just about the whole town had assembled for what was turning out to be the most exciting thing since Scott Martin hit town.

The speck in the distance grew larger, belching steam and smoke like a medieval dragon. By the time the iron horse was a hundred yards away, it had slowed to a turtle's pace, coming to a stop with the second passenger car even with Whiskey River's main street. The conductor was the first to alight. He placed a stool at the foot of the steps and rushed up to help a passenger disembark.

There was pushing and shoving as everyone craned their necks to catch a glimpse of the new arrival. A gloved hand reached out from the recess of the car's vestibule. The conductor took it and guided a shapely woman down the steps and onto the street. He disappeared up the step and returned with two carpetbags that he placed beside her. He tipped his hat to her and signaled to the engineer. Two short blasts and the train slowly chugged away.

The solitary figure, smartly dressed in a light blue, form fitting outfit, with matching gloves and heavily veiled hat, was the object of intense conjecture, as she faced the sea of curious onlookers.

Jake made his way to the front of the crowd and there was

recognition as he peered through the veil. Jake's face betrayed nothing. He muttered something to her and hefted the two bags. Every eye was glued on them as they strolled to Jake's house.

·   ·   ·   ·   ·

"Right about here is where I took the slug in my arm. I had just said to Jake . . ."

Scott's words hung in mid-air at the sound of the train whistle.

Billy, with a quizzical look, said, "Didn't know the train stopped her anymore."

Scott's smile was a rueful one. "Only to throw deadbeats off, " he remarked. "Come on let's go see who's getting tossed off this time."

Billy shook his head. "I'm not up for another rousing Whiskey River welcome."

"I hear you, man. Let's get Jake's wagon up on its wheels and be on our way to Santa Fe."

Chapter Sixteen

No one saw the train disappear over the western horizon. All the attention was fixed on Jake and the mystery woman. Speculation was rampant as the ladies gathered in front of the Emporium.

"Well, Jake certainly seemed to know who she is. Although he did look a bit surprised," one biddy offered.

"Probably one of Teresa's Mexican kin from Texas," Mrs. Gladstone pronounced with the authority of her self-proclaimed leadership position.

"The way she was covered up, how could you tell?" Henderson's wife dared to ask.

"All those Mexicans look alike," Mrs. Gladstone replied with a frosty stare.

"Well, whoever it is, she sure didn't want us to know. I wonder why that is," Mrs. Henderson said as she retreated behind the counter.

"I guess we'll find out soon enough," Mrs. Gladstone said, "but I hope she hasn't come here to stir up trouble. We've had enough of that what with the row that's brewing between that drifter, Scott Martin, and those two hoodlums that work for Sam Hardin."

All heads turned in Fred Henderson's direction when he said, "Maybe we've seen the last of that drifter. Saw him riding out of here right after lunch with that Injun that caused all the ruckus this morning. Looked like he had all his belongings tied on to the back of his saddle."

Marjorie Perkins, who had been silent up until then, tossed in her two bits worth. "And good riddance I'd say. It's bad enough we have to put up with that Snake Weston's strutting around here like he's so special."

·   ·   ·   ·   ·

It wasn't until she was inside the house that Jake's guest removed her hat and gloves. Teresa stared at her as if she were a long lost friend come back to life. When she finally found her voice, Teresa gushed, "Sakes alive, Sarah Chandler, what a surprise. I thought I'd never see you again, especially after we didn't hear from you for so long. You never answered any of our letters."

It was Sarah's turn to be surprised. "What letters?"

Sarah and Jake exchanged glances. "You mean to say you never got them?"

Sarah shook her head. "No, Teresa, not a one."

Teresa rushed to embrace her. "Oh, Sarah, how awful. I can't imagine what horrible things you must have thought about us." They cried, they hugged some more and wore out two handkerchiefs apiece before they were done.

"Oh, Sarah, why didn't you keep in touch with us? You know we would have done anything for you."

Sarah dabbed at her eyes once more. "I felt if there was anyone I could count on to let me know what was really going on, it would have been you two, but when I didn't hear from you, I just assumed you all were part of the whole mess."

"Sarah, how could you?"

"I know. I'm so ashamed."

"Well, enough of that kind of talk. What in the world brings you here after all these years?"

"I'll get to that in a bit. What about you two, and who is this lovely young lady?"

Teresa took Laura by the hand and said with immense pride, "This is Laura, the daughter we thought we'd never have."

"You don't mean . . . you're not saying Doc Carver was wrong. That you were able to have children after all?"

Sarah cocked her head to one side and added, "But, it can't be. It's only been sixteen years, and she's no sixteen-year old."

"No, Doc wasn't wrong. This is Laura Randle, and you're absolutely right, she's no sixteen-year old. She's been living with us since she was four. Her mother was Abigail Randle, who Sam Hardin married shortly after you left. When she died in childbirth, we took her in as Abby asked us to, and she's been the joy of our life."

Sarah stiffened at the mention of Sam Hardin.

Laura's curtsy was impish. "I am so pleased to meet you, after hearing so much about you, especially in the last week."

"Oh," Sarah remarked, "and why would that be?"

"Since that Scott Martin hit town, he's got the whole place stirred up," Laura replied.

"Who is this Scott Martin and what does that have to do with me?"

"Just a guy who drifted into town and got Sam Hardin and his two thugs all riled up," Jake cut in. "I gave him a place to stay in the livery in exchange for helping me out until his foot mended."

"But, that doesn't answer my question."

"Sarah, this may not be easy for you but you're going to hear it sooner or later, so you might as well hear it from me. We believe it was Sam Hardin who put his two hoodlums up to shoot Jesse, but until somebody can prove it, ain't nothing going to change."

Sarah gasped and covered her mouth and chest at the same time. Teresa ran to catch her when it looked like she was going to collapse. She eased Sarah into a chair, while Laura fetched a glass of water.

Sarah took a few sips from the glass and handed it back to Laura. "Oh my God, what have I done?"

Teresa and Laura exchanged perplexed looks.

"You haven't done anything," Teresa said. "None of this is your fault."

Sarah continued to shake her head. "If only I'd . . ."

"If only you'd what?"

"Nothing, Nothing. Tell me some more about this Scott Martin."

"Well, just that he's got the whole town worried, because they don't know what to make of him. The way I see it, if they weren't feeling guilty about something, they wouldn't spend so much time worrying about him," Jake said.

"I think I'd like to meet him."

"Well, he took off for Santa Fe with a friend who showed up out of nowhere. Says he's coming back in about a week, but you know how fiddle-footed those saddle tramps can be," Laura said as she strode from the room.

• • • • •

In less than an hour Sam Hardin summoned Snake Weston and Marv Culpepper to his office. "What can you tell me about the woman who got off the train today?"

"You know as much about her as we do," Snake answered in a tone that could best be described as indifferent.

"Damn it man, that's what I'm paying you for . . . to find out things like that."

"Lookie here. The train stops. She gets off. She's covered from head to foot. Nobody gets a gander at her face. Jake Morgan ups and takes her to his house. There ain't nothing more I can tell you."

Sam Hardin steepled his fingers under his chin and squinted at Snake. "I hear Jake Morgan is making accusations you murdered Jesse Chandler. Why do you suppose that's coming up after all these years?"

"I don't get paid to think about things like that. I get paid to keep the town I line, that's all."

"Some things are getting out of line, and you and your pal don't seem to be able do anything about it."

"What things?" Snake asked.

"Like letting an Injun sashay into town and make a fool of you."

Snake's face darkened and his eyes became slits. "I'da had that redskin dancing back to his wigwam if'n that stable hand hadn't sneaked up on me from behind."

"Seems to me that's the third time he's handed you your balls on a tray. Is that how you keep him in line?"

"He's gone ain't he? Him and that Injun took off and from the looks of things, he ain't coming back."

"What gives you that idea?"

"He took all he owned with him, including one of Morgan's horses and saddle."

"Well, you've got your head up your ass if you believe that. Jake Morgan may not be the sharpest person in these parts, but he's not dumb enough to let a man ride off with a hundred dollar horse without expecting to see him again."

"Trust me, Sam. That jasper knows he's got to face me sooner or later, and he's too yellow for that, I'm telling you he ain't coming back."

"You better hope he doesn't, because if he does, one of you is going to end up dead, and I ain't inclined to bet against that Martin feller."

"He's had his chances. He just decided to hightail it out of here with Morgan's horse and saddle to boot," Snake said with his ever-present sneer.

Hardin scratched his beard and stared at the ceiling before leveling his gaze on Snake. "What would you say if I was to tell you that I just found out this Martin feller has a five hundred dollar bounty on his head, dead or alive?"

Chapter Seventeen

Teresa placed two heaping spoons of tea in the tea ball, screwed on the top and dropped it into the steaming kettle to let it steep while Sarah put out the cups and spoons.

"It's been a long time since we shared a pot of tea and gossiped the afternoon away, Tere."

"It's been quite a while since anyone called me Tere. Too long."

Teresa dried her hands on her apron and shot Jake a meaningful look. "Don't you have to shoe a horse or fix a wagon or something?"

"No, I got nuthin . . . "

Teresa arched an eyebrow and cleared her throat.

"Uh, yeah I do have to fix the hinge on the corral gate," Jake muttered and excused himself.

After Jake left, Sarah said, "I see you still brew your tea the way that English Major showed you . . . 'take the tea to the kettle, never the kettle to the tea' . . ."

Teresa finished the line, "otherwise the kettle will go off its boil."

They both laughed like two schoolgirls at their imitation of the major's British accent.

"It's so good to see you, Sarah, and good to see you laugh. This whole mess must have been hard on you. I'll mind my own business if you tell me to, but I never could understand what it was that made you pick up and go with nary an explanation."

Sarah studied her hands in her lap as she spoke. "Looking back on it, I guess I did act impulsively. At the time I felt so ashamed I just wanted to get out of here."

"Good heavens, Sarah, what in the world are you talking about, ashamed?"

Sarah looked up, her eyes boring into Teresa's. "In the sixteen years since I left here I haven't breathed a word to anyone about what I'm going to tell you. You've got to promise me you'll never repeat it to anyone, not even Jake."

"You have my word, Sarah."

"Long before I left, Jesse and I were drifting apart. I wanted children, but he just kept spending more time working the ranch. We didn't have fights or anything like that, we just weren't intimate. We made love now and then, but there was no more romance in our marriage. When I got pregnant with Lucas, I thought he'd change, you know, spend more time at home, but the baby seemed to drive us further apart."

"I didn't know he was that set against having children, Sarah."

"I don't know that he didn't want children, it's just that he didn't let anything come between him and building up the ranch. I even wanted to name the baby Jesse, but he wouldn't hear of it. So, I named him Lucas, after the uncle who left me the property."

Teresa cocked her head to one side. "So, it was after your uncle. I always thought it was a biblical name, after the apostle San Lucas."

"Maybe a little of both. You're forgetting my maiden name is Martinez."

"I see you haven't forgotten your heritage . . . and your faith."

Sarah shook her head. "My heritage no, but I don't know about my faith. You have no idea how much I prayed, I guess God's plans didn't coincide with mine."

Teresa threw her head back and laughed. "You want to know how to make God laugh? Tell him your plans."

A rueful smile played at the corners of Sarah's mouth. "I sure wish he'd tell me his."

"Never mind his, what are your plans?"

"I really don't know, Tere. I guess I had to find out whatever happened to Jesse. After all, he's still my husband. All Sam Hardin said in his letter was that he got shot over a card game and that he took over the property in settlement of Jesse's debts. I don't even know if Jesse is living or dead."

"What about the ranch? You going to let him just take it away from you like that?"

"The hell with the ranch. Let Hardin have it. It's what ruined our marriage. It did something to Jesse. It became an obsession with him. Everything had to be bigger and better than anything else. Back in Kansas City we were happy, me teaching school and Jesse working for the railroad." Sarah looked away, her eyes misting once again.

Teresa removed the kettle from the stove and poured the tea. "We can take this up later. Let's talk about more pleasant things."

•   •   •   •   •

While the two women in the house were getting reacquainted, Jake and Laura put halters on the wagon team and led them out the barn. When he came back for the horse he was going to ride, he said to Laura, "As soon as you saddle up the paint, we'll be on our way. I'll wait for you outside."

Laura shook out a saddle blanket and said, "I'm glad you asked me to go with you. Things have gotten dull around here since Scott took off for Santa Fe."

"He did liven things up a mite, but I expect he'll be back soon enough"

"You think so?"

"He said he would."

"We'll see," she said, more to herself than to Jake as he led the gelding from his stall. When she tried to place the saddle blanket on the paint, it whinnied softly and shied away. "What in the world, has gotten into you?" Laura murmured.

She tried again, but the horse snorted and backed away.

"What's the matter? You don't want to go to Devil's Pass? Is that it? You think something bad is going to happen again?"

Laura led the paint back to its stall and said soothingly. "Don't worry sweetie, I'll take the roan. She doesn't know what happened up there." Then she paused and eyed the paint skeptically. "Unless you two been talking . . . have you?"

The roan was in the adjacent stall with a window that opened out toward the street. Laura was about to slip the bit into the roan's mouth when she heard an angry voice from the front of the livery. She quietly hung the bridle on its peg and cracked open the wooden shutter.

"So, Jake Morgan," Snake said, "you running a livery stable or a boarding house for every stray that comes into town?"

Jake looked at Snake the way he'd look at a cockroach before he stepped on it.

Snake's face hardened. "I asked you a question, Morgan."

Jake took off his hat and reached in his back pocket for a bandana. He wiped the perspiration from his forehead and the inside band of his hat before putting it back on. Only then did he answer Snake. "I'll be glad to tell you, if you can tell me what business it is of yours."

"I'm making it my business, and you'll tell me who the lady visitor is if you know what's good for you."

Laura felt her pulse quicken. She wheeled around and ran to what Jake called his office. She jerked a chair from the other side of the room and stood on it to remove the double barrel shotgun hanging on an exposed ceiling beam. She pressed the release, broke the gun open to make sure it was loaded before hurrying back to the window. She gave an involuntary gasp when she saw Snake's hand move to his gun.

Over Snake's shoulder, Jake caught a glimpse of the shotgun that Laura propped on the windowsill. He deliberately folded the bandana and put it back in his pocket "That's always been a problem for me, Snake. I don't always know what's good for me. Why don't you spell it out?"

The pistol jumped into Snake's hand, or so it seemed. He pointed it at Jake's belly button and said, "I ain't so good at spelling either, so I let this do my talking for me. Now, tell me what I wanna know."

Jake nodded. "That puts me at a disadvantage. You see, I don't have a pistol to talk for me like you do, but you know Laura Randle? Sam Hardin's stepdaughter? Well, she can be pretty close mouthed herself at times, so she lets her shotgun do her talking. Matter of fact she's got it pointed at your back and it just might start yammering away if you don't put that pistol back where it belongs."

Snake's eyes narrowed. He hesitated between sneaking a peek over his shoulder and taking his eyes off Morgan. Finally he said, "Nice try, Morgan. I'm going to count to three and if I don't get no answer out of you, I'm gonna put a bullet in your knee."

He thumbed back the hammer and counted, "One . . two . . ."

During the pause between "two" and "three" the ominous sound of two clicks broke the silence when Laura cocked both barrels of the scattergun.

The sneer on Snake's face turned to rage.

Jake folded his arms and gave him a patronizing smile. "What we have here is what you call a Mexican standoff. Nobody wins and nobody loses, unless you're dumb enough to think Laura won't squeeze those triggers. Matter of fact, I'm willing to bet she's hoping you'll do something that'll give her cause to."

Snake glared at Jake with his pistol pointed at Jake's belly. "Ain't much of a man lets a woman do his fighting for him."

Jake continued in his condescending tone. "You ever see what two loads of buckshot can do to a man from that distance? It ain't a pretty sight. It leaves a mean and oozy corpse."

Snake released the hammer and dropped the Colt into its holster. "OK, Morgan," he muttered "like you say, it's a standoff. You won't be so lucky next time."

"That works both ways, tinhorn."

Laura released the hammers on the shotgun and joined Jake in the street. Watching Snake Weston retreating to Sam Hardin's office, she asked. "What was that all about?"

"Either that idiot has a curiosity that's gonna get him killed or Sam Hardin can't stand not knowing who our guest is. One way or the other, I expect things are gonna get touchy real soon."

Chapter Eighteen

The sun was warm on their backs as Billy and Scott crossed the bridge over the Santa Fe River. At the other side Billy said, "Well, *amigo*, from here on in you're on your own."

"What do you mean? Aren't you coming with me?"

"You kidding? Ain't nobody going to rent an Indian a bed for the night."

"But, I need you to show me around, Billy. I'd get lost in a big town like this."

"This ain't Kansas City, Luke, er Scott. Just follow this road and it'll take you to the main square, the Alameda, and you'll see the Palace of the Governors on the north side. That's a good starting place for what you gotta do. To the east of the square, about a couple of hundred yards is La Posada de Los Reyes, The Kings' Inn. Not fancy, but it should be in your price range."

"I wish you'd stay in town with me, Billy."

"Easy for you, paleface, but you're crazy if you think I'm welcome there. Besides, there's someone I gotta see."

"I think we can work around that. There's bound to be a back entrance. You know, the one all the self-righteous town fathers sneak out of after a roll in the hay with their chippies?"

"I don't follow you."

"I'll register for both of us, get the keys for the rooms and meet you on the second floor. Lop off that hair and you can pass for Mexican any day."

"Who knows? My father is probably Mexican. But, what if somebody spots me?"

"First thing take that headband off and put my hat on. If anybody says something, just mumble something in Spanish."

Billy gave him a wry look. "My Spanish isn't that good."

"For God's sake, Geronimo speaks Spanish, how come you don't?"

"Because he was an Apache, born in Mexican territory. Besides a lot of good it did him . . . the Mexicans almost did him in along with his band of warriors."

Scott threw his hands up. "You're just as stubborn as ever. But before you go, I'd like you to do something for me. Ask around if your people know what happened to Jesse Chandler. From what I hear he was friendly with the Navajos and was always good for a steer or two when buffaloes were scarce."

"That's exactly what I plan to do. There's a person at the Mission just west of town who just might be able to help us. Meet me there when you're done. I think you'll find her very interesting."

"Her?"

Billy gave him a mischievous smile. "You'll find out."

•　　•　　•　　•　　•

"Sarah, it's been two days since you arrived and you haven't set foot out of this house once. You're going to have to face them sooner or later."

Sarah sighed wearily. "I know . . . I'm just working up the nerve. What am I going to say when people start asking a whole bunch of questions?"

"Just tell them you've come to take your ranch back and run that thieving Sam Hardin out of the territory. That should start their tongues wagging."

"I told you, Tere, that piece of property brought me nothing but grief and heartaches. Let the bastard have it."

"Look at me, Sarah, this is Tere you're talking to. That property had nothing to do with it, and you know it. It's something else and whatever it is, you've come back to put it to rest."

"Oh, Tere, I've been so miserable. I wish I had never come

back. Why couldn't I have just left things the way they were?"

"Because, you're like a coyote caught in a trap. You'll die if you don't free yourself, and the only way to free yourself is to chew your leg off. Either way it's going to be painful, so start chewing."

• • • • •

After ten hours of sleep and a breakfast of *huevos rancheros*, *frijoles refritos*, and *café de olla*, Scott was ready to start drawing the noose around Sam Hardin's neck. His first stop was the courthouse.

"Señor Valera?"

"Yes, Armando Valera at your service."

"Thank you, Señor Valera, the desk clerk at the hotel told me that you're the person to see. I'm representing the owner of a piece of property to the south of here. I have the last will and testament of the original owner who received the land under a Spanish land grant, as well as the deed of ownership that was recorded. The owner is thinking of disposing of the property and wants to verify that the title is good and clear of any encumbrances."

Mr. Valera, obviously of Mexican descent, examined them closely and said, "Everything appears to be in order, but this transfer of property took place over twenty years ago. I'll have to search the records to make sure that this title is still valid. The fee for that is one dollar."

"How long will that take?"

Valera shrugged. "About four or five days."

Scott's jaw dropped. "That long?"

Valera eyed Scott the way a hustler sizes up a rube at county fair. "There is a special fee for rapid service, if you need it sooner than that."

"How much sooner?"

"It depends on the level of service."

Scott recalled something he heard a long time ago about Mexicans and their dread of knives. A pistol didn't frighten them nearly as much as a knife. One bullet and they were dead, but death from knife wounds was agonizingly slow and painful. Scott slid the Bowie knife from his waistband and while cleaning his fingernails said in a low voice, "Don't push your luck, *amigo*. Tell me what the fee is for really special service, and I'll tell you if we have a deal."

Beads of sweat broke out on Valera's forehead as he stared nervously at the knife. He licked his lips, cast a furtive look around the room and said hoarsely, "Twenty dollars."

"Ten, and you get your money when I see the records."

The clerk hesitated.

Scott grabbed him by his shirtfront and pulled him close with the point of the knife lodged under his chin. "And ten more to forget all about this conversation, or I'll come back and cut out your tongue."

Abruptly, Scott's scowl turned into a magnanimous grin. He released his grip and shook the clerk's hand warmly. "A pleasure indeed. You've been very helpful. Then I'll see you this afternoon around . . .?"

"Uh . . . three . . . yes, three will be fine."

•　　•　　•　　•　　•

Following the directions the desk clerk gave him, Scott covered the short distance to the office of the U.S. Marshall in ten minutes. He also learned from the desk clerk that the marshal was seldom in his office before noon, time enough for Scott's gambit. He grasped the wrought iron door handle, took a deep breath and pushed the door open.

The office was sparsely furnished with a wood desk and swivel chair on the right, a gun rack on the wall to the left, and a ponderosa pine trestle table with four ladder-back chairs against the rear wall. Tacked to the wall behind the desk was a clutter of notices, handbills, and "Wanted" posters.

The old-timer with tobacco stains on his gray beard looked up from his sweeping. He worked his jaws briefly and scored a bull's eye with his stream of tobacco juice. He wiped the dribble off his chin with his sleeve and fixed Scott with a baleful stare. "Can I help you with something?"

"I'm looking for the Marshall."

The old-timer drew the back of his hand across his lips and cackled, "Usually, its tuther way around."

Scott acknowledged that bit of wry humor with a nod and a grin. "I reckon. Do you expect he'll be in soon?"

"Hard to tell. Marshall McCabe don't keep no regular hours. You welcome to wait."

Scott consulted his watch and said, "I guess I can hang around a spell. Mind if I check your 'wanted' posters?"

The old-timer stopped to fire another salvo at the spittoon and squinted at Scott. "You one of them bounty hunters?"

"Nah, just had a run in with an hombre in Whiskey River and was wondering if he might be wanted for something, somewhere."

"Look all you want. When you done there, there's a stack of old ones on that table by the wall. Me, I got to work to do. The name's Bart if you need me."

While Bart went about his job of moving little piles of dirt from one side of the room to the other, Scott examined the artists' sketches on the wall. The faces had one thing in common . . . they were all mean and ugly with small beady eyes and cruel lips. No one can be that mean, Scott thought. Then a mental image of Snake Weston formed in his head and he reconsidered.

When Bart put down his broom and shuffled off to the back room, Scott moved over to the table where the older handbills were stacked. He flipped through the stack and had gone through half of them when one caught his attention. He held up the yellowed piece of paper and examined it carefully. The unmistakable face of Russ "Snake" Weston glared back at him. With his back to the rear of the office, Scott folded the poster, slipped it into his shirt pocket and left quietly.

Chapter Nineteen

"Sarah, while Laura and Jake are up at Devil's Pass fetching the wagon, let's you and me sashay to the Emporium and give this town something to talk about."

"Like you said, Tere, I have to do it sooner or later, but I don't think I was this nervous the day I got married."

"That settles it. Get your purse and hat and let's go before you change you mind."

* * * * *

The emporium was more than a general store, it was the communications center of Whiskey River, although factual reporting was seldom a consideration. In regard to Morgan's mystery guest, however, a new standard was established for wild speculation. It ran from the absurd to the outrageous.

As usual, Hester Gladstone was the clarion of misinformation. "Well, I'll tell you, whoever that person is, if she has nothing to hide, why won't she show her face? The good Lord only knows what awful things she's done."

Marjorie Perkins picked it up from there. "Exactly, what are we supposed to think, the way she stays shut up in that house?"

"Ladies, let's not be so hasty in making judgments," Fred Henderson said. "I'm sure there's a reasonable explanation for everything. After all the Morgans are upstanding, God fearing people."

Mary Henderson sniffed. "If they're such upstanding citizens, how come they take in such riff raff like that Scott Martin?"

"Did I hear someone question my morals and integrity?"

Every head spun in the direction of the new voice. The gasps were audible at the sight of Teresa and Sarah standing in the doorway.

Teresa graced them with a syrupy smile. "Oh, don't let us interrupt your little hen party. I'm especially interested in what else you have to say about me."

Teresa turned to Sarah and said, "You see, Sarah, I told you there was nothing to worry about. These are the same sweet, kind, loving people you knew when you lived here."

"Sarah? Sarah Chandler? Is that really you? Land o' Goshen, what in the world brings you back after all these years?" Mary Henderson asked.

"To stir up more trouble, no doubt," Mrs. Gladstone spat. "Just like that no good Scott Martin. I don't know why some folks just can't leave well enough alone."

Their harangue was cut short by the gravelly voice of Doc Carver who had slipped in unnoticed. "Tell me, ladies, just what awful things has this riffraff, as you call him done? Seems to me he's the only refreshing thing that's happened to this town in quite some time. Those two hooligans, Snake and Marv, have goaded him into fights from the day he set foot here, and all he's done is make jackasses out of them."

Doc paused, cocked his head to one side, and continued, "No that's not exactly right. Those two come by their jackassedness naturally. They were born that way. Scott just removed any doubt people may have had."

Hester Gladstone glared at Doc Carver. "You're a fine one to talk, with your head stuck in a bottle . . ."

Doc cut her off. "You may be right about my affection for the booze, but it doesn't cloud my sense of justice. Besides, what right do you have to pass judgment on people? When all of you sold your silence to Sam Hardin, you lost your right to condemn anyone. On the other hand, at least you made out better than Judas. All he got was thirty pieces of silver . . . you got several hundred acres of land."

Hester Gladstone, her face contorted in rage, screeched, "So that's what this is all about. A conspiracy to take away from us the land that's rightfully ours."

Sarah, visibly shaken, shook her head. "You don't understand. It's not about the land. It's . . ."

Hester Gladstone's lip curled in a contemptuous sneer. "What else could it be? You run off and leave your husband, a good man who worked his heart out for you and his child, and now you think you can just show up and take back what isn't yours anymore. I'm sure Sam Hardin will have a lot more to say about that. Ladies, I think we should go. I'm tired of being lectured by the town drunk."

Doc bowed in acknowledgment. "Some people drink to forget. Others, like your husbands, because they're married to hags like you. Go on, go back to your dungeons and your cauldrons of lizards and frogs."

Sarah, in shock, and Teresa, convulsed with laughter, watched their enraged exodus.

Doc Carver nodded pensively. "We haven't seen the last of them. They'll be back for their brooms."

•　　•　　•　　•　　•

Later that same day Scott closed the lid of his watch and stepped inside Mr. Valera's office.

"Good afternoon," Scott said cheerfully. "I trust you have the information I need."

Armando Valera got up to meet Scott at the door. "This was more difficult than I imagined. There are complications," he said in a low voice.

"Indeed," Scott said, "and what kind of complications are we talking about?"

"The property in question is still in the name of Sarah Chandler, but a Mr. Samuel Hardin has filed a claim to the property based on two issues. One in settlement of a debt and the other the fact that Mrs. Chandler has abandoned the property. You see, Mr. Martin, according to the terms of the Spanish land grant, the recipient is obligated to improve the land, foster the creation of a community, and promise to defend it against all enemies. Since Mrs. Chandler abandoned the property, Hardin claims she has forfeited her right to it."

"That may be true," Scott said, "but I have done some research on this matter and the Treaty of Guadalupe Hidalgo guarantees ex-Mexican citizens their property rights. When New Mexico became a territory of the United States, all conditions established under the original land grant are no longer applicable."

"I see you have done your homework, Mr. Martin, but what about Mr. Hardin's claim on the basis of the money owed him?"

"That also is illegal. The property is in Sarah Chandler's name. Sam Hardin took her property to satisfy her husband's personal debt, which, by the way, has not been substantiated and which he has no legal right to do."

Valera appeared dubious. "Although Mrs. Chandler has a good case, there are intangible factors that could weigh against her."

Scott's eyebrows shot up. "Intangible?"

Valera drew Scott away from the door and continued in a whisper, "The settlement of many of these disputes has been influenced by the generosity of the petitioners. If Sam Hardin is a man of such means, the judges could easily be . . . let's say, be influenced. And the fact that he has lived on the land for fifteen years, is no small consideration."

"Señor Valera, you have been extremely helpful. You have answered one important question for me. Mrs. Sarah Chandler is still the owner of record of that land. For that I feel I owe you much more than what we agreed on, and I apologize for my behavior this morning."

Valera dismissed the apology with a wave of the hand. "No, you owe me nothing. As you are aware, I am of Mexican descent and at first I thought Mrs. Chandler was just one more gringo who cheated a Mexican out of his rightfully owned land. Now I see that she is also of Mexican ancestry and it is that *gringo hijo de puta,*

Hardin, who is trying to steal her land. A word of advice . . . the best way to fight this is to prove he took over the land through trickery or some other nefarious means. As dishonest as some of our public officials are, they don't want to be tarred with the same brush as the criminal."

Scott palmed a twenty-dollar gold piece in his right hand and pressed it into Valera's hand. "I'm already working on that."

Chapter Twenty

Marjorie Perkins left the Emporium and made straight for Sam Hardin's office. He looked up in surprise when she came bustling through the front door, her lips drawn tight under her pinched nose.

"Marjorie Perkins. What brings you here on such a lovely day?"

"It won't be lovely for long, Sam. Guess who that stranger is that got off the train two days ago. Sarah Chandler, that's who."

Hardin stiffened. "Who told you that?"

"Didn't need anybody to tell me. Saw her with my own eyes at Henderson's."

"Did she say what she's doing here?" Hardin inquired cautiously.

"Not exactly, but when Hester accused her of coming to get her land back, she said it wasn't about the land, but she didn't get a chance to go on, Hester tore into her so. And then Doc Carver showed up and said the most awful things. Not to Sarah, but to us."

"What kind of things?"

"Things I don't want to repeat, but he did warn us that the day of reckoning was coming soon for all of us. What do you think he meant by that?"

"It's hard to tell what an old coot like him means. But, tell me something, how does she look?"

Marjorie cocked her head. "Who?"

"Sarah Chandler."

Marjorie eyed Hardin curiously. "Just as attractive as ever. Galls me to admit it. I secretly hated her for being so pretty, and so nice at the same time. It's a shame the way things worked out. For her, that is," Marjorie hastened to add.

"When did all this take place?"

"Not more than five minutes ago. I rushed right over here figuring you'd want to know straight away."

"Of course," Hardin assured her. After an awkward pause, he continued. "You suppose she's still at the Henderson's?"

"I imagine so. Why? You planning on talking to her?"

Hardin shrugged it off. "Nothing special. I'd just like to know what brings her back here after all these years."

"Humph, we'll find out soon enough, but it seems to me you got more on your mind than that."

· · · · ·

Hardin stared at the door long after Marjorie Perkins ushered herself out. For fifteen years he ruled over his fiefdom . . . his subjects, like chattel, bound to pay him allegiance. What loyalty he couldn't buy, he elicited through intimidation and coercion. Retribution had been swift for the rebellious. The walls of the kingdom were solid and the gates were strong. Now it was under siege. He could sense the enemy closing in, but who was the enemy, he wondered.

How do I fight a foe I can't see? Why, after all these years, does Jake Morgan openly accuse "Snake" Weston of murdering Jesse Chandler? And that bitch, Laura Randle, goading everyone with that smart mouth of hers. Now, all of a sudden, Doc Carver decides to take a hand, not mention the ghost of Jesse Chandler that has continually haunted me without mercy. All of this started the day that sonnuva bitch, Scott Martin, hit town. And now Sarah Chandler pops up.

I hadn't reckoned on that, especially after all these years. What kept her away for so long? And what prompted her to show up now? It couldn't be because of Jesse. That marriage was dead. If she had any feelings left for Jesse, she would have come back as soon she learned he'd been shot.

Hardin dared to ask himself, "Does she think she can rekindle an old fire, if there was any fire to begin with?"

There was a time Hardin thought there was a blaze raging out of control. What else was he supposed to think, the way she responded to him when they made love. And after their love making, they'd excitedly plan their next secret encounter . . . the willow grove by the stream, the seldom used outrider shack on the south forty, the abandoned silver mines. Discovering new hideaways was as exhilarating as the rendezvous. No matter how remote or inaccessible their trysting places, the specter of discovery only heightened their excitement. The taste of the forbidden fruit. Then it stopped. No reason. No explanation. It simply ended.

Like a lovesick cowpoke, Sam couldn't get her out of his mind. He'd invent reasons to ride into town hoping to run into her . . . pass by the schoolhouse where she was teaching just to get a glimpse of her . . . drop in Sam's Emporium and buy crap he didn't need on the outside chance he'd bump into her. Sarah always managed to avoid him. He wondered if Jesse had gotten wind of their affair, but quickly dismissed that notion. Jesse Chandler would have come looking for him and Sam Harding didn't want any part of that.

It must have been Sarah, so consumed with guilt for betraying Jesse. That's when Sam began to entertain the notion of getting rid of Jesse once and for all. With Jesse out of the way, Sarah and all that land would be his.

A year went by and Sam thought he would go out of his mind. He pondered the various ways he would kill Jesse, but in the end Sam knew he didn't have the nerve to do it. That only increased his loathing for Jesse, and for himself, for being so weak. One day, driven to the edge of madness he rode over to the Chandler place to finally get it over with. He was going to confront Jesse and tell him he was in love with his wife, and when Jesse attacked him, he'd shoot him in self-defense. But Sam didn't get the opportunity to tell him.

Jesse was a big man, always held himself erect and walked with a purposeful stride, but that wasn't the Jesse that shuffled to the front gate. His shoulders sagged and his voice showed his weariness when he said to Sam, "Something I can do for you?"

Hardin's survival instincts, not his cowardice, warned him this was not the occasion to tell Chandler that he had come to take is wife away from him. "Just passing this way and thought I'd take a look at that new Shorthorn bull I heard you got."

Jesse shook his head. "Sam I believe it would be better if you dropped by some other time. I've got a lot of other things on my mind."

"Some other time then. Regards to Sarah."

"Not likely, Sam. Sarah's gone."

"What do you mean gone? Has anything happened to her?"

"No Sam. She left me. I come back from a couple of days of rounding up the spring calves and all I find is a note saying she's leaving. Took the boy and that half-breed injun she inherited from her uncle and left. Now, if you'd be so kind as to leave so I can get back to my chores."

On the way to his spread Sam was a tortured soul. *Did Sarah ever have any feelings for me, or was it all about the sex? Sarah was young and attractive with a desperate need to be desired, to be sexually fulfilled, and Jesse wasn't doing the job. Would she ever leave Jesse for me, or was she merely using me to satisfy those needs that Jesse wasn't?*

Then Abigail Randle came along and, more out of spite than anything else, Sam married her, but Abigail was no Sarah Chandler. Every time he made love to Abigail, he imagined it was Sarah. She could never satisfy him the way Sarah did, and Abigail, sensing she was just a surrogate, became more aloof and cold. Eventually whatever affection Sam might have had for Abigail turned into loathing and contempt. That's when he vowed to get rid of Jesse Chandler. Then, maybe Sarah would come back. Jesse would become a memory, but Sarah never came back.

• • • • •

Joshua McCabe looked more like a saloonkeeper than a U.S. Marshall. His short frame with his belly lopped over his belt like a sack of grain hanging from the back of a mule could hardly strike terror in anyone's heart. He eschewed a pistol for a shotgun and as far anyone could tell, he'd never been in a fistfight, but his reputation as a peace officer that knew and upheld the law was known throughout the territory. One glimpse of his steely gray eyes made it clear why this was no man to be trifled with. It was into those eyes that Scott found himself staring when he returned to the marshal's office later that afternoon.

"You the feller Bart says was here earlier?"

"I'm the one."

"Who are you and what's your business here?"

"My name is Scott Martin and I want to swear out a complaint against one Sam Hardin for conspiracy to commit murder." Scott removed the poster from his shirt pocket and laid it on the desk in front of McCabe. "And this is the person he paid to do it."

McCabe studied the poster and replied, "That poster is all the justification I need to bring in this Weston. He's wanted for shooting a deputy in Silver City, but this Sam Hardin, that's a different story. What proof do you have about this conspiracy thing?"

"I have a witness who overheard Hardin when he paid Weston for shooting Jesse Chandler."

"When and where did all this take place?"

"About fifteen years ago in Whiskey River," Scott replied.

"Fifteen years ago! And he's just now coming forward. What the hell has he been waiting for?"

"It's a long story, Marshal. I guess he's just been waiting for someone to persuade him to do it."

"And that's where you come in, I suppose."

"That's right."

"Where the hell you been all this time?"

"Kansas City. Just came to Whiskey River about a week ago."

"What's your interest in this affair?"

"Sarah Chandler, Jesse Chandler's widow, hired me to get her land back from Hardin. That's why he paid that polecat, Weston, to shoot Chandler. He wanted that land, but what he didn't know was that it never did belong to Jesse Chandler. It's always been in his widow's name."

"What do you mean hired you? You some kind of detective?"

"I'm a lawyer and she hired me to investigate the

circumstances of Jesse Chandler's disappearance."

"Wait a damn minute. Is this Chandler dead or simply disappeared?"

"We're assuming he's dead. Nobody's seen him in fifteen years, but I said I wanted file a complaint of conspiracy to commit murder. The fact that we don't have a body does not exonerate Hardin from hiring someone to shoot him with intent to kill."

"Dang, you sure have a flimsy case. One witness who's waited fifteen years to speak up, no body, and a widow who's decided after all these years to boot the alleged culprit off her land. What proof do you have the land is even hers?"

"I've just come from the Palace of Governors where Señor Armando Valera did a title search on the property in question and he assures me that it is still in Sarah Martinez Chandler's name."

McCabe drummed his fingers on the desk. "What I don't understand is how this Hardin feller drove her off her property."

"He didn't exactly drive her off. She had left her husband about a year before he got shot and she only found out about it when Hardin wrote her and said he was taking over the land in payment of her husband's debts."

"I see. So how come she's waited all this time to do anything about it?"

"Like I told you, Marshal, it's a long story."

McCabe spun around in his swivel chair to face the wall and stroked his walrus mustache. Abruptly, he turned to face Scott again and asked, "What's a hell-raiser like Snake Weston doing in a jerkwater place like Whiskey River? From what I hear that town's deader than the twelve apostles."

"They work for Sam Hardin . . . to keep the peace, Hardin style."

"That doesn't make sense to me. Hard cases like that generally take the money and run."

"I've asked myself that same question, Marshal. You see, Sam Hardin doesn't know I work for Sarah Chandler. He thinks I'm some drifter who bounced into town, and he offered me five hundred dollars to get rid of those two hired guns. The way I figure it they're blackmailing him about the shooting."

"Those two?"

"I forgot to mention Weston has a sidekick by name of Marvin Culpepper."

"And Hardin wanted you to . . ."

"Get rid of his problem, as he put it," Scott added.

"What did you tell him?"

"Told him I'd think about it."

"So, what's your plan?"

"Tomorrow I'm going to see a judge and try to get an eviction order."

"And what if the judge won't give you one?"

"Like you said, you got good reason to arrest Weston, and maybe Culpepper too. Once you got them in custody, perhaps you could persuade them to confess it was Hardin who put them up to it. If you hint the judge might go easier on them if they cooperate, they might go for it. After all, without a body, they'll only be facing a charge of attempted murder. They won't swing from a rope for that."

McCabe nodded. "If that don't work, there are other ways. You say they're still hanging around?

"If they're not lazing in the Pearly Gate Saloon, they're strutting around town like they own it."

"What about you?"

"Like I said, nobody knows the real reason why I'm there. I do some work for the owner of the livery in exchange for room and vittles."

"One last question . . . where's the widow Chandler while all this is going on?"

"As far as I know she's back in Kansas City."

McCabe pointed to the poster in Scott's hand. "Don't know if that one thousand dollar reward is still being offered. It's been a long time."

"It doesn't matter to me. I'm not doing this for the reward. I just want to see my client get her land back with Weston and Hardin behind bars."

"Tell you what . . . give me a couple of days and me and one of my deputies will mosey on down to Whiskey River for a look see. It would help if you'd be there to point him out to us. Just make sure this Weston doesn't get wind of it."

Chapter Twenty-One

Doc escorted Teresa and Sarah across the street to his office. Once inside he tossed old journals and empty bottles on the floor to make room for them to sit, making no apology for the chaos.

"Now you see how an old reprobate lives, but why bother tidying up? It's sort of like an eternal Purgatory. Can't move on until I'm purged of my sin, and my sin's too grievous to forgive. So, I just teeter between heaven and hell till they make up their minds who's gonna come get me, God or Lucifer."

"Hush up that kind of talk, Doc Carver," Teresa scolded. "You're a much better man than you give yourself credit for. There's many a person in this area who wouldn't be alive today if it weren't for you, and most of them still owe you for it."

Doc Carver opened the side drawer of his desk and reached for one of the bottles stashed there. He stared longingly at it, then on second thought put it back and closed the drawer. "I'd offer you ladies a drink, but the only thing I have is some of MacPhearson's sorry imitation of good liquor. If I had a teapot I'd make some tea, if I had some tea. So let's dispense with the amenities and get right down to brass tacks. What the hell you doing back here Sarah?"

"To be honest with you, Doc, I don't really know. I've been by myself for too many years now. It gets so lonely," she said dabbing at her eyes with a handkerchief.

"Damn, look at me blubbering like some school girl. You remember Luke, my son, well he left home a little over three years ago. Said he was going to study law in Chicago. And the Indian boy, Billy, he never did adapt to city living and upped and left about five years before that. I got to thinking about Jesse and just had to close that chapter for good. For God's sake, I don't know if I still have a husband or if I'm a widow."

Teresa looked skeptical. "Is that the only reason, Sarah?"

"What other reason would there be?"

"What about the ranch? With people starting to flock out here, it could bring a pretty penny."

"I couldn't care less about the ranch. Hadn't been for that miserable piece of land, we'd still be happily married and raising a family in Kansas City."

"Call it woman's intuition, Sarah, but there's something you're not telling."

Sarah fell silent and avoided Teresa's eyes.

"Sarah," Doc said gently, "I understand your loneliness, and I agree, you've got to put an end to the doubt. If Jesse's alive, you have to pick up where you left off. A new start. I know how much you loved him, and how much it must have hurt to have to leave the way you did. I'll help you any way I can."

"You know, Doc, you've been one of the few people I could talk to. You've always been so understanding, but there were things you can't even imagine."

"Don't think I'm just a whiskey soaked old fool. There ain't much goes on I don't know about. I know more than you think."

The fleeting look of panic that crossed Sarah's face wasn't lost on Teresa.

Doc, seated behind his desk, shifted to one side and rearranged his lanky frame. "When's the last time you saw Luke?"

"Let me see, must have been over a year, maybe a little more."

"What kind of man did he grow up to be? What's he look like?"

Sarah's face softened and her voice filled with pride. "Oh, he's a handsome young man. About six feet tall, sandy hair and impish gray eyes. He has smile that would charm the bark off a tree."

Teresa's hand shot to her chest as she and Doc exchanged glances.

"What does he think of your coming here?" Teresa asked.

"I haven't discussed it with him. He doesn't know."

"Where is he now?"

"In Chicago, I imagine."

"Tell me, Sarah, how does Luke feel about Jesse?"

"He used to ask about him all the time. Wanted to know why his daddy didn't want him."

Teresa nodded. "What did you tell him?"

"I told him his father loved him very much, but I couldn't bring myself to say he was dead, so I said that he just disappeared."

Doc cleared his throat. "Now wouldn't that be some coincidence if Luke were to show up here, just like you did, looking for his daddy?"

This time Sarah's look of panic was more than fleeting.

●　　●　　●　　●　　●

That night back at his ranch Sam Hardin slouched in the overstuffed chair facing the fireplace, a bottle of whiskey dangling from his hand. He raised it to his lips, took a hard pull and grimaced as the fiery liquid seared his throat. He closed his eyes and waited for the warm, mind dulling glow to surge through his body. Ever since Sarah Chandler left, this had become his daily routine. The only difference between him and Doc Carver was Doc made no attempt to hide his addiction.

Every evening, for fifteen years, he would sit in that chair and drown his dream in a maelstrom of alcohol . . . the dream of Sarah Chandler gracing the mansion with her beauty, as his wife. Sam was not a passionate man, but Sarah Chandler aroused in him a lust he didn't think possible. The vision of Sarah and him making love on the bearskin rug in front of the hearth drove him to the brink of madness. All he could think of was that Jesse Chandler didn't deserve a woman like Sarah, so warm, tender, and sensuous. Only he could satisfy the longing in her soul and the desire of her flesh. But Sarah wouldn't leave Jesse, and Sam's jealousy drove him to think the unthinkable . . . Jesse had to die. But, what went wrong? With Jesse dead, why did Sarah stay away?

In a spate of fury, Sam heaved the empty bottle into the fireplace. It lay shattered in a thousand pieces, just like his dream. Then he stared at the dying embers and cursed silently. *She's been here three days and hasn't even tried to get in touch with me. So what's she here for?*

All Sam knew at that moment was that he had to have her. One way or another Sarah would be his again.

·　　·　　·　　·　　·

A lot of things changed when New Mexico became a territory of the United States, but one thing remained constant, the influence of its Mexican heritage. At exactly six the next morning, the sound of church bells from the other side of the Alameda filled the hotel room . . . a call to the faithful to come and worship. Scott, shaken from a deep slumber, awoke with something other than prayer on his lips. "What the hell . . ." he groaned.

The early September sun, still obscured by the Sangre de Cristo mountains, had not yet penetrated the gray dawn. Scott groped in the dark for a match in the drawer of the nightstand. He scratched it into flame with his thumbnail and lit the stub of a candle in the terracotta candleholder. He peered at his watch in the flickering light then stumbled to the window to see what could possibly be going on at that time of the morning to cause such a ruckus. Women with brightly colored *rebozos* over their heads and a few old men were the only signs of life as they converged on the church for morning Mass.

Momentarily disoriented by the unfamiliar surroundings, he filled the basin with water from the porcelain ewer and buried his face in it. The cold water shocked him out of his somnolence and helped clear away the cobwebs. *Santa Fe. Hotel room. Marshal McCabe. Supposed to see the judge today.*

Between the time he dressed and sat down for breakfast in the dining room, Scott revised his agenda. He decided to wait until after Marshal McCabe's visit to Whisky River before entering a petition for an eviction order. If Snake Weston and Marv

Culpepper, to save their own hides, implicated Sam Hardin, there wouldn't be any need for it he reasoned. McCabe would have everything he needed to arrest Hardin and put him away for a very long time.

The tomato and onion omelet laced with *jalapeños* and a side of *chorizos* put his musings on hold. After washing it down with two cups of strong black coffee, he pushed away from the table eager to hit the trail and find out what awaited him at the mission where Billy was expecting him.

·　　·　　·　　·　　·

The sun had scaled the mountain peaks, but a chill lingered in the morning air. Scott felt the warmth of the rising sun as he headed west to La Mision de San Francisco. He was in no hurry so he let the Appaloosa find its own gait. The trail followed a series of bends and switchbacks along a stream until it dropped down to the small valley where the mission was located. Nestled among a grove of cottonwoods and willows, the adobe walls of the mission blended perfectly with the surrounding terrain. Prickly pear cactuses, their fruit ranging from bright red to deep purple, provided the only splash of color in the drab setting.

Scott dismounted and pulled the bell rope hanging at the opening in the adobe wall, then led his horse in the direction of the main building. Before he got to the entrance, a monk appeared out of nowhere and greeted him.

"Welcome, brother. Peace be with you."

Scott removed his hat and replied, "Thank you. This is indeed a peaceful place."

The monk acknowledged the compliment with a smile and a nod. "What brings you to the San Francisco Mission?"

"I have a friend, Billy Bear Heart, who told me to meet him here. Do you know him?"

"Indeed I do. He is a frequent visitor. If you will wait here, I will find him for you. You may tie up your horse over there in the shade of the trees."

Scott watched the monk disappear around the side of the building and wondered at his remark about Billy's being a frequent visitor. "Why," he asked himself, and then added, "I'll ask him myself. There he is now."

They embraced with the traditional Spanish *abrazo*. "So Luke, you found your way here."

"Watch it Billy. The name's Scott. Remember?"

"Yeah, I forgot. I just can't get used to it. Hope I don't let it slip out at the wrong time."

"Maybe this thing will be over sooner than you think, and I can drop the charade."

"Does that mean you got the eviction order?"

"Better than that. I found out that varmint, Snake, is a wanted man and the Marshal's going to mosey on down to Whiskey River and take him in. I'm betting he'll squeal on Hardin to save his own skin."

Billy broke out in a wide grin. "Oh, man, is Sarah going to be happy to hear that!"

"I don't know, Billy, she has no idea what happened to Jesse. She probably still thinks he got shot cheating at cards."

"Well, don't you think you ought to tell her? There's a telegraph office in Santa Fe."

"I think I'll wait until we got him dead to rights. No sense in raising any false hopes. Besides, I'd still like to find out what happened to my father before I notify her."

Billy's face grew somber. "I think we can put that worry to rest."

Chapter Twenty-Two

Billy led Scott to a graveyard behind the chapel and stopped in front of a grave with a wooden head marker. Scott removed his hat and read the inscription carved in the wood slab.

"J. Chandler died July 9, 1861, R. I. P."

He dropped to one knee and traced the letters with his finger and let it linger on the space between the J and the C.

"The S is missing, Billy. His middle name is Scott."

"So that's where your new name came from. And the Martin?"

"From my mother's maiden name, Martinez."

Scott got to his feet and reached for his bandana to blow his nose.

"Scott, you going to be all right?"

"Now I am. You see, Sarah never told me he had been shot. She only said he disappeared, I never could understand that . . . why he never sent for us or came and got us. Somehow, I always blamed myself. Hell, I was just a kid and I figured it was something I said or did. The only thing I could ever think of was to find him and show him I wasn't such a bad kid after all. I wanted him to be proud of me."

"Scott, I'm sure he was very proud of you. It must have been something else."

Scott's shoulders sagged. "I reckon I'll never know. Learning he'd been shot, helped some. At least it explained why he didn't come for us, but even after Jake Morgan told me about Snake Weston's shooting Jesse, I still held out hope that I would find him alive. There is so much I wanted to tell him . . . to ask him."

"Suppose I leave you two alone for a spell so you can tell him now. He's surely with the Great Spirit, and I know he's listening. I'll be back after a while."

Scott edged closer to the grave and rolled and unrolled the brim of his hat. He swallowed hard a couple of times and licked his lips with a dry tongue. When he spoke, all his tight, parched throat could produce was a hoarse, "Pa." He wiped his eyes with his shirtsleeve and tried again. "Pa . . . Mom always told me how much you loved me, but I thought she was just telling me that to make me feel good. I wanted to believe her, but I kept asking myself how could that be true, if you just ran out on us. I kept blaming myself. All these years the only thing I could think of was to show you what a good son I was."

Scott sniffed and wiped his eyes again. "Now doggone it, I'm so damned mad, but you'll never know that, 'cause you went and got yourself shot. And I'm angry at myself too . . . 'cause I hated you so much all these years, and now I'm sorry you're dead and I can't even tell you I'm sorry 'cause you can't hear me."

Scott looked up a the sky and shouted, "Well, I'm sorry, you hear? You hear that? I said I'm sorry." Then he bowed his head and let the tears wash away his anger . . . his pain. The next thing he knew Billy was standing next to him with his arm around his shoulder.

Scott put his hat on and said to Billy, "I'm thinking something. How do you know that's really Jesse Chandler in that grave?"

"Because there's someone here who saw him the day he showed up half dead from his bullet wound. You may want to hear what she has to say."

Billy took Scott by the arm and steered him toward an area behind the stable where the monks raised a variety of small animals. Just east of the main building there was vegetable garden where two of the monks were harvesting the early fall vegetables. In the distance, several milk cows grazed in the lush grass along the stream that branched off from the Rio Grande just outside of Santa Fe.

An Indian woman, who Scott guessed to be in her fifties, came out the back door of the main house with a letter in her hands. She looked questioningly at Billy, who nodded. She handed the letter to Billy, said something in Navajo to Scott and gave him a hug.

Scott, caught by surprise, halfway encircled the woman with his arms before he let them drop. He then gave her a half-hearted, awkward hug before backing away. He looked to Billy for explanation, who simply grinned at Scott's discomfort.

Billy spoke in Navajo, "Scott, this is Rosario. She goes by her Christian name. I told her you speak some Navajo."

"So, you are the one whose father is buried over there. What is it you want to know?" Rosario asked.

Scott shrugged and made a helpless gesture. "I guess I just want to be sure it's really my father. What can you tell me?"

Rosario pointed to the front of the monastery. "It was late one afternoon, many years ago, and I was raking leaves when a man, badly hurt, rode through the front gate. He fell off his horse when he reached the entrance and I ran to help him. His shirt was soaked with blood and he was having difficulty breathing. In his hand he was clutching this letter. I ran inside and called to Padre Juan who came out with some of the other monks and helped get him to a bed. He could barely talk and his skin was gray. He had lost so much blood."

Rosario stopped and cocked her head to one side before going on. "I remember him saying, 'It's too late for me, but I want to make sure my wife gets this. Her name is Sarah Chandler. She lives in . . .' then he died before he could finish."

Rosario stopped, took the letter from Billy and handed it to Scott. "Billy says you are this man's son. I'm sure the contents will prove that you are."

Scott's fingers trembled as he took the letter. He started to open it, then stopped.

"Aren't you going to open it?" Billy asked.

"No, it's not for me. It's for Sarah."

"Yeah, you're right. But, at any rate I guess it answers your unresolved questions."

"As far as my father is concerned, yes, but one thing I don't understand is how did you know Rosario had this letter?"

"I didn't. I found out two days ago when I told her about meeting you in Whiskey River and how your father was shot."

"Some coincidence," Scott said.

"It's no coincidence, Scott. It is the Great Spirit who led me here to find my mother, just as he guided you to the grave of your father."

Scott's eyes grew wide. "your . . . your mother? But I thought you were an orphan . . . that your mother was dead."

Billy moved to the woman's side and put his arm around her waist. "I thought so too, but when I was working as an interpreter for the Army, I found out differently, but I'll tell you about that later. She lives here at the mission. She cooks and helps look after the animals."

"How did she end up here?"

"Her parents were casualties of the fighting between the "yellow hairs" and the Indians. An army captain found her wandering alone and took her to the mission where she was raised by the nuns. When she was older, she went to work for a large landowner as a domestic and when he died she came back here."

"I see," Scott said to Rosario, "You must be delighted to be reunited with your son. I am very happy for you. I'm also happy for Billy. He and I were very close."

Billy snorted, "Closer than you think."

"What do you mean by that?"

"We're cousins."

Scott's head snapped back. "What? What do you mean cousins?"

"That's right cous. Besides the letter Jesse left there's a family bible that Rosario kept all these years. It belonged to Don Lucas Fernando Martinez, the uncle who left your mother his estate. It explains everything. When Don Lucas's wife died, Rosario took over the running of the household. Two years after Lucas's wife died and your folks took over the estate, she came back to the mission and left me in the care of the Chandlers, because she wanted me to have all the advantages of the white man's world."

Billy took the bible and showed Scott where all the Martinez family births and deaths were recorded. "See, here's Sarah, listed as the daughter of Lucas's brother, and this is when his wife, Isabel, died. Two years after Isabel's death, I was born, and here I am, the son of Lucas Fernando Martinez and Rosario. All the others are dead, except Sarah and me."

Scott shook his head in amazement and gave Rosario a lopsided grin and said, "It looks like we're related some way or another, but darned if I can figure it out."

Rosario was beaming. "For a long time, Billy was the only family I had, even though he was in Whiskey River and I was here. When he moved away, I thought I'd never see him again. But now he is back."

Scott tucked the letter in his pocket, tipped his hat to Rosario and said, "I guess I better get this to Sarah. But, first I got something to say to my father."

•   •   •   •   •

Back at Jesse's grave Scott removed his hat, knelt on one knee and scooped up a handful of dirt. "If it weren't for Sam Hardin, I'd be talking you in person instead of to a head marker," he said aloud. He studied the reddish soil in the palm of his hand and went on. "But I guess this is all that's left of you, except for some dried up bones. I say it's time we evened the score."

He got to his feet and let the dirt sift through his fingers. He watched it form a small pile at his feet before putting on his hat saying, "Sam Hardin, you sonnuva bitch, you better pray Marshal McCabe gets to you before I do."

Scott found Billy waiting at the hen house. "Got some things to settle in Whiskey River, Billy. You coming?"

"I wouldn't miss it for the world."

Chapter Twenty-Three

Two and a half days at a steady pace brought Scott and Billy to La Quebrada del Diablo, where the narrow cut lay in the shadow of the steep walls of the arroyo. At the entrance Scott reined in his horse and removed his Winchester from the saddle holster and levered a cartridge into the chamber. Billy pulled up alongside and asked, "Why the artillery? You counting on trouble?"

"I doubt it. No harm in being prepared though."

Billy gave him a skeptical look. "Prepared for what?"

"Just a feeling that things are coming to a head and who knows what has taken place in the week we've been gone."

"Sure seems like it's been more than a week since we came through here," Billy said and then added, "Time sure flies when you're chasing desperados."

"Talking about time flying, it ain't more than a couple of hours to town, and that's when the fun begins."

Scott urged his horse into the entrance and the rode in single file until they came to the spot where the wagon had been. "Looks like Jake's been here for his wagon," Scott observed.

Billy pulled up alongside. "Well, that takes care of Jake's problem. Have you figured out how you're going to handle yours?"

"I've been thinking about that ever since I left Santa Fe and I've decided as much as I want to get this over with, it's best to lie low until the marshal gets here."

Billy had a dubious look. "What if he doesn't? I mean that wanted poster's over fifteen years old."

"He will. Lawmen have long memories when it comes to gunning down one of their own."

"Just the same . . . what if he doesn't?"

The lines around Scott's mouth tightened. "In that case I'll have to take him myself."

"Then why wait for McCabe? Do it now. Shoot the skunk the way he gunned down your pa. You got every right, him being a wanted man and all."

"You don't get it Billy. It's Hardin I want. Snake may have pulled the trigger, but it's Hardin who put him up to it. There's nothing Hardin would like better than to see Snake dead. Shit, he even offered me five hundred dollars to take him down. Snake's the only person who's holding something over his head. With him out of the way, Hardin is as free as butterfly."

"Well, get Snake to talk then."

"What's he going to gain from that? He'd be admitting he killed him in cold blood. He'd be signing his own death certificate."

"Then I guess we just wait for McCabe to show up."

"That's right. We'll head straight for Jake's livery where I told him I'd wait for him."

· · · · ·

At the same time Scott and Billy arrived La Quebrada Del Diablo, Laura and Sarah were chatting idly at the kitchen table. The conversation covered every inane subject imaginable . . . the weather, the inhabitants, how the town had changed or hadn't changed. Without admitting it, they were all avoiding the one topic foremost in their minds. Abruptly, Teresa irritated at the senseless chatter, said, "Sarah, you can't spend the rest of your life moping in my kitchen. You're going to have to make up your mind what you're going to do."

"You think I don't realize that? The problem is I don't know what to do."

"For God's sake, Sarah, Hardin paid that Weston feller to kill Jesse. The whole thing was rigged. On top of that he stole your land, and you're going to let him get away with it?"

Sarah banged her clenched fists on the table. "Hardin didn't kill Jesse. I did. Jesse's dead because of me," she shrieked.

"What in tarnation are you talking about?"

"Tere, I was going out of my mind. I loved Jesse so. I was young, in love, and I needed him to want me . . . to make love to me, but he just ignored me. I tried everything . . . coaxing, teasing, even pleading . . . but he was always too tired, too busy, or too . . . you name it. You have no idea how desperate and lonely I was."

Sarah looked away, then buried her face in her lap as the tears fell in torrents. Her body shook as she sobbed uncontrollably.

Teresa spoke softly. "Sarah, I had no idea . . ."

Sarah lifted her head. "It was more than that. I felt so alone . . . if I'd had a child it would have been different. I would have had someone to make me feel needed, someone to share my love with, but there was nothing but that big ugly, lonesome house. It was because of that I started flirting with Sam Hardin. He was charming, considerate, and he made me feel like a woman . . . like was I was attractive to men."

Teresa stared open mouthed. *No, this can't be. Sam Hardin of all people. How could she? No wonder she's so wretched.*

"But Sarah, how could you?"

"Tere, I didn't mean for it to go any further than that, but . . ."

"But what?"

"He filled a void in my life. My head kept telling me it was wrong, but my heart wouldn't listen. He said all the right things . . . the things I needed to hear. With Jesse I was beginning to wonder if it was me . . . if I wasn't pleasing to him, or to anyone . . . I didn't know what to think. Sam made me feel alive, desirable, pretty. I honest to God don't know where my head was, but we started out just seeing each other. Oh, there was excitement in sneaking around, but I never thought it would go any further than that, but the next thing you know we kissed, and I just couldn't stop myself from there."

"Sarah, I never had an inkling. How in the world did you manage to keep it a secret for so long?"

"Oh, we were very careful. Went to places people seldom went. Like a line shack the outriders didn't use anymore. One that Sam fixed up so it was nicer than the rest. He even kept extra clothes and food there. We made sure we were never followed. What a dumb, foolish idiot I was."

Laura spoke up for the first time. "No as big an idiot as I was."

Sarah and Teresa's heads snapped in her direction. "What! You mean . . . you're not going to tell us that Sam Hardin . . ."

Laura's dark eyes smoldered, unable to hide the fury seething within. Her full lips parted as she took a deep breath. "No, Sam didn't seduce me, if that's what you're thinking, but that doesn't mean he didn't try. At first I believed him when he told me how much he loved my mother and how sorry he was she died the way she did. Told me how much he missed my being around the house, and how he would like me to come back and live with him."

"Laura," Teresa asked, "when did all this take place?"

"About five or six years ago . . . I must have been around seventeen."

"Why didn't you tell us?"

"Oh, he was charming, all right. He really seemed sincere, and I was almost ready to move back there. He invited me to the ranch to see what he'd done to the place. He said he wanted to show me the room he had fixed up for me. Stupid, innocent me, I believed him and rode out there on a Sunday afternoon, when most of the hands were in town."

Sarah shook her head in disbelief. She envisioned the whole scene being played out, just as it did when Hardin enticed her into his lair. *That depraved bastard, how could he? Laura was just a child, his stepdaughter for God's sake.* She shuddered as she contemplated the kind of man who would do such a thing.

"Well, he showed me the house and when we got up to my room, he put his arm around my shoulder, kind of fatherly like, and asked me how I liked it. I don't remember him showing me any affection when I was little, but I didn't pay it much mind. I mean I was impressed and he seemed so anxious to please me. Then he dropped his arm to my waist, spun me half around and pulled me towards him. Then he put his other arm around me and pulled me so close my breasts were mashed against his chest. He was holding me so tight I could hardly breathe and he bent over and kissed me hard on the mouth."

Teresa's eyes were blazing. "That no account slimy bastard. What else did he do?"

"It took me by such surprise, I didn't realize what was happening. Then all of a sudden he let me go and said he was sorry, that he didn't know what came over him. It was just that I reminded him so much of Abigail, he lost control."

"And that was that?" Sarah asked.

"That's all that happened . . . then. Later when I was ready to leave, he insisted I stay a while longer . . . 'have some lemonade' he said. He seemed so ashamed of himself I kind of felt sorry for him so we sat down on that big davenport in front of the fireplace. Next thing I know he's running his fingers through my hair telling me how much I reminded him of her. Something inside me told me to get up and run, get out of there, but I couldn't move I was so scared."

Teresa put her arm around Laura. "Poor child, you must have been petrified. What happened next?"

"Then he started talking about how sad and lonely he was since Abigail died and how much he loved her, all the while he was trying to unbutton my blouse. All of a sudden I remembered Doc Carver's telling me how my mother wouldn't have died if Sam Hardin had sent for him sooner. How he just stood there and watched her die. Here was the man who could have prevented her from dying trying to seduce her daughter. I don't know exactly what happened next, but I remember getting so mad . . . I was furious."

"Dear God," Sarah exclaimed, "what did you do?"

"I managed to break away from him and he lunged after me. I stumbled backwards and tripped on the hearth. I reached behind me to break my fall and my hand fell on a brass poker from the fireplace. I grabbed it. I only wanted to threaten him with it. I didn't mean to hit him with it, but he kept coming at me. And his face . . . you can't believe the look. It was the most frightening thing I ever saw. It was hideous . . . no, it was evil. I took the poker in both hands and screamed, right before I cracked him across the shins with it."

Teresa stared at Laura. "Is this true? I mean, of course it's true, but it's so repulsive."

Laura, her eyes blazing as if she were reliving the episode, spat out, "Damn right it's true, and my baby brother died along with her. He murdered my mother just like he murdered Sarah's husband. If he hadn't fallen to the floor, I truly believe I would have kept hitting him . . . and hitting him . . . and hitting him . . . until I killed him."

Teresa reached across the table and took Laura's hands in hers. "But you didn't and that's OK. You did what you had to do. He had it coming to him. It's over now."

Laura pulled her hands back. "You don't understand. It's not over. Every time I think of him, every time I see him I wish I had killed him. I taunt him every chance I get hoping he'll give me cause to finish what I was too frightened to do back then."

"Laura, you mustn't think that," Teresa said.

"You didn't hear the vile names he called my mother and me when he fell to the floor after I hit him. I'm sorry, Sarah, it was unkind of me to say what I did about Hardin killing Jesse, but the truth be told, Sam Hardin is a wicked man and no one here is man enough to stand up to him. I'd like to know what kind of hold he has on everyone. For a while I was hoping Scott would be the one to settle his hash, but it looks like he's taken off with that Indian friend of his and it's not likely we'll see him around here again."

Sarah stopped twisting her handkerchief and spoke firmly to Laura. "I'll tell you what kind of hold he has. I've come to realize that Sam Hardin is like a snake. He poisons his victims leaving them paralyzed and helpless. For fifteen years I've let his venom ruin my life, but not anymore I'm purging myself of the poison . . . the poison of shame and humiliation. You see, until I do, Sam Hardin still controls me. Well I have decided to take control of my life. I now know I can spit in Sam Hardin's eye and cleanse myself of the remorse and mortification I've lived with these past fifteen years. You have to do the same thing. Don't you see, Laura, until you do, you're never going to be at peace."

"I'll be at peace when that son-of-a-bitch catches a bullet in the heart," Laura said vehemently.

"Laura, listen to me, you're young . . . you're beautiful . . . you have so much capacity for love. Don't let hatred embitter you."

Sarah got up and began to pace in measured steps. She'd stop as if to say something, then shake her head and resume her methodical pacing between the front door and the kitchen. Ultimately she stopped, folded her arms across her chest and said, "Laura, would you saddle up a horse for me. I think a long ride in the hills will help clear my head. Give me time to sort out what I need to do."

•   •   •   •   •

Sarah held the reins of the roan while Laura gave one final tug on the saddle cinch and adjusted the stirrups for Sarah's height. "All set to go. She's a gentle horse and knows her way around. Just let her have her head in the hill country."

Sarah placed her left foot in the stirrup and swung stiffly into the saddle. She reached down for Laura's hand and said, "You can tell I haven't done this in quite a while. Thanks for the loan of the riding skirt. I never was one for side saddle."

"Think you can still find your way?"

Sarah laughed. "There are some things you never forget . . . and some things you'd like to."

"Sure you don't want company? I don't like the looks of that sky. It's getting pretty dark," Laura said with some concern.

"I'll be all right."

"At least take a slicker with you in case you get caught in a rain."

"That won't be necessary. I won't be going far. Just want to get out of town for a while. Anyway, you said the mare knows her way. I'll just let her bring me home."

Chapter Twenty-Four

The sun, now obscured by rapidly forming clouds, was overhead when Billy reined in his horse about a hundred yards north of the railroad tracks at the edge of town. "You sure you want to parade right up main street with me tagging along?" he said to Scott.

"Why not? We're kin, aren't we?"

"Yeah, but those palefaces don't know that. As if that would matter," he threw in as an afterthought.

Scott chuckled at the irony of the situation. "They're going to find out soon enough."

Billy shook his head. "Just the same, I'd rather take another route. I ain't exactly inconspicuous."

"What are you afraid of, Billy?"

The stubborn set of Scott's jaw was nothing new to Billy. Arguing would be useless. What always worked best was the "dumb Injun" approach. "Scott, tell me once more why you want the marshal to take Snake Weston alive."

Scott heaved a deep sigh and said wearily, " I thought I made that pretty clear."

"Well, you got me confused. I thought the whole purpose of bringing the marshal in on this was to take Snake alive so he can squeal on Hardin. But, if we have a run-in with that hothead and you end up shooting him, doesn't that kind of mess up your plan?"

Scott clamped his jaw even tighter and squinted at Billy. Grudgingly, he turned his horse to the right and growled, "We'll follow the tracks to that wooded area yonder and cut through it to the other end of town."

Billy nodded his approval. "Why didn't I think of that?"

Scott shot him a sidelong glance and broke out laughing. "Billy you were always smarter than me. You never failed to get me to do what you wanted and make it sound like my idea. That's one of the things I missed most after you left. You were my big brother."

"I hate to disappoint you," Billy said, "but it turns out we're cousins now."

•   •   •   •   •

Jake was hammering out a new linchpin for the wagon tongue when movement from the wooded area behind the corral caught his eye. He set it aside to cool and observed two riders emerging from the trees. By the time he walked to the back door of the stable Billy and Scott, still holding the rifle, had dismounted and were hurriedly leading their mounts inside.

"Well, I see you two got back all right. Some folks were betting we'd seen the last of you."

"Sorry to disappoint them," Scott said.

"Some won't be . . . one of 'em leastways."

Billy saw Scott's face turn crimson and sang in a barely audible voice, "Scott's got a girl friend, Scott's got a girl friend."

Scott wheeled and glared at Billy, while Jake nodded knowingly.

"Expecting trouble?" Jake asked, pointing to the rifle in Scott's hand.

Scott examined the Winchester like he was wondering how it got there. "Not exactly, but trouble seems to follow me wherever I go."

Jake grunted. "It's more like you bring it with you, if you ask me."

Scott shrugged. "You might be right . . . at least this time. I'm bringing some real trouble . . . trouble for Snake Weston, that is. Found out in Santa Fe he's a wanted man."

"How in hell that come about? I thought you and your friend here were going to Santa Fe to kick up your heels."

"Well, yeah, but I got this notion that somebody like Snake must have a bounty on him. So, I went to the Marshal's office and he shows me a bunch of old posters and sure enough, there he was."

Jake scratched his chin. "Can't say I'm surprised. What's he wanted for?"

"Shooting a deputy in Silver City about fifteen years ago."

"So what's your next move?"

Scott flipped the stirrup over the saddle and loosened the saddle cinch. "Wait for the Marshal."

"What Marshal?"

The cinch fell free and Scott lifted the saddle off the Appaloosa. "Marshal Joshua McCabe. When I told him Snake was in Whiskey River, he said he'd come on down to take him in."

Jake removed the saddle blanket while Scott placed the saddle on a rail. "And when is this going to take place?"

"Any day now . . . who knows maybe even today." Scott said.

Jake nodded several times. "You sure have been a busy man in Santa Fe. What else you been up to?"

"Some other stuff, but I think Teresa and Laura might want to hear it also."

"There's someone else might want to hear it too."

Scott removed his gloves and shoved them in his back pocket. "That a fact? Like who?"

Jake hung the blanket over a rail and said ever so casually, "Someone who got off the train the day you two left."

Scott and Billy exchanged glances. "That's right," Billy said, "we did hear the train whistle while we were working on your wagon. Did somebody else get the heave-ho?"

"No. This time she got off under her own power."

Scott failed to conceal his surprise "She?"

"Yep," Jake went on in the same matter of fact tone, "took everybody by surprise. Some folks are plenty anxious over it."

"What the hell are you talking about? Anxious over what?"

Jake stopped what he was doing and looked intently at Billy, then at Scott. "I'm talking about Sarah Chandler. She's come back."

Billy maintained his stoic expression. Scott's eyes narrowed and he cocked his head to one side. "You sure? Sarah Chandler,

Jesse Chandler's widow?"

"In the flesh."

"What the hell is she doing here?"

"She didn't say."

"Where is she now?"

"Went for a ride. Laura saddled up the mare for her."

"A ride? Hope she don't plan on getting too far from town. Looks like a storm could be brewing."

"Don't rightly know. You'll have to ask Laura. She and Teresa are up at the house fixing lunch."

The events of the past few days had pushed Laura to a remote corner of Scott's mind, but at the mention of her name, he found himself rubbing his jaw where she socked him the night before he left.

"You think it's safe for me to go there, Jake?"

Jake laughed. "You'll be in heap more trouble if you don't go."

•   •   •   •   •

From the day Sarah Chandler returned to Whiskey River, Sam Hardin couldn't get her out of his mind. When he was in town, he kept a vigil at the window of his office hoping to catch a glimpse of her, but after her hateful reception at the Emporium, Sarah hadn't ventured out of the house again. Given that the unwelcome mat was always out at the Morgan's, he readily dismissed that option. He thought about sending her a note, but that was too impersonal.

As each day passed, he became more obsessed with seeing her. When he wasn't at the ranch ranting at the foreman, he closeted himself in his office drinking more openly and freely. His foreman, weary of the scorching tirades over the most trivial things, upped and quit and half the ranch hands were ready to join him. Even the townspeople, normally deferential to his whims, began to shun him. Snake and Marv were the only ones who made no effort to avoid him, a further measure of their lack of good sense.

On the sixth day after Sarah's arrival, Sam Hardin stood at the front window looking out onto the street, his ever-present glass of whiskey to his lips. He almost choked when Sarah Chandler rode by his office. He stepped out on the front porch and followed her with his eyes until she crossed the train tracks, heading out of town. He licked his lips, slapped his hat on his head, and slipped out the back door where his horse was tethered. He made his way along the back alley until he crossed the railroad tracks and veered to his right and followed Sarah from a discreet distance.

•   •   •   •   •

Snake and Marv, seated on the verandah of the Pearly Gate, observed Sarah as she rode by with more than casual interest. "Say Snake, ain't that the gal that's got Sam in such a tizzy?"

"Don't know about that, but this much I do know, he sure ain't been the same ever since she got here."

"You think maybe there was something 'tween those two and that's why she hightailed it out of here?"

"The way she's been holed up in that blacksmith's house, something must've been going on."

Marv let out a long low whistle. "Well, lookee there. Ain't that the boss man I see riding out of town?"

Snake stood and peered after the figure disappearing beyond the tracks. "Looks like him to me."

"Hey, Snake. What do you say we kind of tag along and see what he's up to?"

Snake cast an eye at the darkening sky and said, "I believe I'll just set here high and dry. Besides, we don't get paid for that, Marv. Anyway, if Sam has on his mind what I'm thinking, I don't think he wants or needs our help. Know what I mean?"

"I believe I catch your drift," Marv said with a lecherous grin.

•　　•　　•　　•　　•

Laura's heart took off at full gallop when she saw Scott strolling up the walk with Billy and Jake. She took off her apron and called to Teresa, "Look who's coming for lunch."

Teresa joined her at the front door. "My Lord, when did you two slip back in town?"

"Slipped in is right." Jake said. "They sneaked up on me like an Ind . . ."

Jake glanced at Billy and stammered, "I mean like. . ."

"You mean like Scott when he sneaked up on those *pistoleros* last week?" Billy said with a straight face.

"Yes. No, dammit, man, you got me . . . never mind, you know what I mean."

"Take it easy. Billy's only funning you," Scott cut in.

Teresa stepped away from the door and thrust her hand out to Billy. "Enough of this palaver. The pump is on the side of the house. You can wash up there and come on in when you've washed off all that trail dust."

Scott doffed his hat, nodded to Teresa and said to Laura, "I told you I'd be back. Surprised?"

Laura felt her face grow hot. "I was, but not now."

Teresa broke in before she had a chance to recover. "Go get cleaned up. Besides there are more important things to talk about."

"You mean like Sarah Chandler?" Scott asked.

Chapter Twenty-Five

Sarah let the mare have her head, not caring where she took her. At one point she stopped and searched for familiar landmarks, but there were none.

"They're all gone. Or have I forgotten where they were? After all, it's been over fifteen years. Some of these trees were saplings the last time I came through here."

Unconcerned she pushed on. She touched her heels to the mare's flanks and resumed a leisurely pace along a path she thought she recognized. After a few minutes she broke out of the trees and off to the left she recognized the old homestead. There was a new sign over the front gate, the Lazy-H. Sarah pulled up and stared longingly at the familiar structure. Her eyes moistened and her throat tightened.

"A couple of rooms have been added on, probably by Sam, but other than that it looks pretty much the same as the day I left. I wonder what it's like inside. I remember how I fussed over the place. Drove Jesse mad. He must have moved every piece of furniture we had twenty times at least. Everything had to be just

right . . . the curtains, the linens, the garden, the pictures . . . throughout it all Jesse was so patient until . . . until what? What happened? What made him change all of a sudden? What was it?

I thought I was going to be so happy here raising a family and helping build a future for us. Funny how things worked out. I gave it all up for what? Barely getting by on a school teacher's pay, no husband, no family, and my only child . . . off to God knows where, doing who knows what. DAMN THAT SAM HARDIN! DAMN ME FOR BEING SUCH AN IDIOT!

So, Jesse wasn't the romantic type. He was a good man, hard working, and solid as a mountain, But, no, I wasn't satisfied with that. I wanted more and what did I end up with" A broken heart and enough remorse to last an eternity."

Sobbing uncontrollably, Sarah dug her heels into the roan's side and flailed at its neck with the reins. The startled animal bolted at a full gallop and headed in the direction of the darkening sky. At the edge of a grove of cottonwoods, a bolt of lightning snaked its way through the black sky and struck a tree immediately to Sarah's left. Her skin tingled and the hair on her neck stood straight out a millisecond before a tall pine tree split down the center followed by a deafening crash of thunder. In one continuous motion the spooked horse shied to its left and reared. Sarah instinctively leaned forward causing her head to smash against the pommel of the saddle and fall heavily to the ground. She lay face down in an unconscious heap while the mare stood silent guard over her in the torrential rain.

•   •   •   •   •

The conversation during lunch was strained. Teresa, Laura, and Jake were busting out to hear about Scott's adventures in Santa Fe, while Scott was equally anxious to her about Sarah Chandler. The light banter persisted until everyone was finished and the dishes were cleared. At that point Jake made a pronouncement, "Scott here says he found out Snake Weston is a wanted man, and that a U.S. Marshal is coming to take him in."

Teresa turned away from the sink and dried her hands on her apron. Laura abandoned what she was doing and both took their seats at the table.

"How in the world did you find this out?" Teresa asked.

"Like I told Jake this morning, I was just curious and stopped in the Marshal's office to see if they knew anything about him, but the truth is . . . what I mean is, whatever I tell you, you'll know it's a lie the minute Sarah Chandler walks in that door."

"What's Sarah got to do with it?" Laura asked.

Jake patted Laura's arm and said, "Let him talk, honey."

Before Scott could continue, Teresa smiled knowingly and

said, "Jake and I figured it out this morning, Luke."

A bemused Billy folded his arms and sat back in his chair waiting for the fun to begin. Teresa prompted Scott with a nod of her head. "Well, are you going to tell her, or shall I?"

"Tell me what?" Laura exclaimed. "What the dickens's going on?"

Scott took a deep breath. "To begin with my name is not Scott Martin. It's Lucas Chandler, but all I've ever been called is Luke."

Laura's reply was drenched in sarcasm. "Except when they call you Scott."

Scott winced at the barb.

"But, Scott . . . damnation I don't know what to call you," Teresa said.

"I guess it doesn't make much difference any more, but, I'd just as soon keep it Scott until things settle . . ."

"I think what Teresa wants to know, and so do I," Jake interrupted, "is why the hoax? Why didn't you just come to us in the first place? Sarah knows she could trust us."

"First of all, Sarah . . . I still haven't gotten used to calling my mother by her first name . . . has no idea I'm here. Secondly, she seldom talked about Whiskey River and I didn't know who was her friend and who wasn't. She could never bring herself to believe that Jesse was dead. In fact, all she told me was that he had disappeared after a shooting over a card game."

Scott looked away and took several deep breaths before continuing. "I don't remember much about my father, but from as far back as I can remember, I was consumed with finding him and settling some issues I had with him. That's why I came to Whiskey River."

Laura's voice lost some of its edge when she said, "What's so unusual about that? That's no reason to get yourself thrown off a train."

"I didn't want to arouse any suspicions. I figured if it looked like I landed here by accident, nobody would give me a second thought. That way I could nose around and find out what I was looking for unmolested. And that's all I would have done, if those two dung balls, Snake and Marv, hadn't tried to persuade me to vamoose. That got my curiosity up and by then Jake told me he overheard Hardin paying off Snake for shooting Jesse, I made up my mind to get to the bottom of it."

"And I thought you were going to Santa Fe to have a good time," Laura said not without a bit of remorse.

"Didn't mean to deceive anyone, but I wanted to find out who was the legal heir to Jesse and Sarah's land."

Scott lifted his water glass and drained it, while others sat on the edge of their seats.

Laura couldn't stand the silence. "So, what did you find out?"

"A lot more than I bargained for. The land is still legally Sarah's but Jesse's dead."

Laura let out a gasp. "Dear God. How awful, I'm so sorry."

Teresa made the sign of the cross. "*Maria santissima, ruega por nosotros.* How do you know this?"

Scott nodded toward Billy. "He took me to his grave."

"Oh, Scott, that must have been so hard for you," Laura said.

"How long have you known about this," Teresa asked Billy.

Billy shrugged. "I found out a day before Scott did. It's a lot more complicated than you think, as you'll find out from Scott. For now, let's just say that my mother felt it was wiser to say nothing."

"Your mother? What's your mother got to do with this?" Teresa asked.

Billy took a deep breath. "I said it's complicated. Let's just say for a long time I thought I was an orphan, but discovered about ten years ago that my mother had been raised in a Mission outside of Santa Fe. Years later she had me, but left me in my father's care and returned to the Mission where she helps out. While Scott was in Santa Fe, she told me how Jesse showed up half dead one night. They buried him there after he died."

Laura reached for Scott's hand. "That must have been such a shock. I'm so sorry, really I am. I've been pouting about your lying to me when all this time you've had so much on your mind."

Scott squeezed her hand. "Yes, it was a shock, but it was more painful not knowing. We had quite a conversation at the graveyard, him and me. I was able to say some things I'd been holding onto for too many years."

"That's good, Scott," Teresa agreed, "don't do you no good to carry grudges around you can't do anything about. They just eat at your innards. You've got to get on with your life."

"I plan to do just that, Teresa. I unloaded a lot of baggage in that bone yard. It's all behind me now."

"How did we get sidetracked?" Jake asked. "Scott started off telling us how he discovered Snake was a wanted man."

"That's right," Scott agreed. "I told Jake this morning it was by pure accident, but the truth is I went to see the Marshal to swear out a complaint against Sam Hardin for conspiracy to commit murder. When I found out Snake was wanted, I figured if we could get him to admit Hardin put him up to it, we'd have a much tighter case. So, Marshal Joshua McCabe is not only coming to arrest

Snake for shooting the deputy in Silver City, but to take him in as a witness in the conspiracy charge."

"What makes you think Snake's gonna talk?" Jake asked.

"Snake's looking at a long time in prison for shooting the deputy. McCabe and I are betting he just might be willing to settle for a lighter sentence in exchange for his testimony."

"What if Snake doesn't go peaceable like and they have to take him back to Santa Fe slung over the back of his horse?"

"We've got make sure that doesn't happen."

"Just how does McCabe plan to carry this out?"

"He said he'd meet us at the livery when he gets here and work out a plan after he sees the lay of the land."

"Which is when?" Jake asked.

From where Scott was sitting he could see the front of the livery. When two men rode up and disappeared inside, Scott said, "About right now."

Chapter Twenty-Six

When Sarah pulled up at the edge of the clearing with the Lazy-H sprawled before her, Sam Hardin felt his pulse quicken. He also reined in his horse and studied the slender figure that sat motionless gazing at what used to be hers . . . and what could be hers once again. He became impatient to see her face, the face he had dreamed of for more than a decade, but the overhanging branches and the darkening sky made that impossible. For now he could only imagine it. No matter, there was plenty of time for that. "After all, why else would she ride out here by herself," he reasoned, "if not to see me?"

His vanity would allow no other explanation . . . Sarah was irresistibly drawn to him. It was that simple. The notion that Sarah had finally come back to him was so overpowering it electrified his fantasy and ignited a raging fire in his loins.

That fantasy was shattered when, without warning, Sarah dug her heels into her horse's flanks and rode away from the Lazy-H in a frenzy, headed for the tree covered hills to the west. Hardin was stunned. Anticipation turned into rejection. Lust became rage. He drove his spurs in his horse's side and took off wildly after her.

The clouds of dust raised by the terrified mare made it easy for Hardin to follow her, until the rain began to fall. Softly at first, but rapidly turning into a gully washer. The sudden downpour wiped out all trace of Sarah's tracks. The rain pouring from the brim of Hardin's hat, like a miniature waterfall and the incessant streaks of lightning that zigzagged their way to earth made following her impossible. In his fury Hardin drove his horse relentlessly up one trail and down another. Sarah had disappeared.

Hardin pulled up about a hundred yards from a wooded area, the last place Sam Hardin wanted to be during a lightning storm, but Sarah, his Sarah, beckoned to him. He nudged the horse forward, but it balked. His spurs raked the horse's sides, but it reared and spun away from the trees. Under the merciless punishment of Sam's quirt, the steed reared once again before plunging ahead. At the edge of the woods, Hardin dismounted and led his horse into the trees where he found Sarah lying motionless, her face covered by her long black hair. Her horse, its reins hanging to the ground, stood solitary vigil over her.

Hardin knelt beside her and brushed away the wet hair revealing a bruised cheek and a large lump on her forehead. He took off his coat and placed it over her while he contemplated his next action. He slowly got to his feet and eased up to Sarah's horse and took it by the reins. He loosened the saddle cinch enough to allow him to pull the saddle so that it was partly hanging on the horse's side. Next he led it to the edge of the trees, pointed it in the direction of town and took out his pistol. A sharp whack on the animal's rump and two shots fired in the air sent the animal in a frenzied gallop in the direction of Whiskey River.

•　　•　　•　　•　　•

"Good afternoon, Marshal. This here is Billy Bear Heart, my cousin, and this is Jake Morgan the owner."

At the word "cousin" Jake gave Scott a quizzical look.

McCabe nodded to Billy and shook Jake's hand. "Joshua McCabe, and this is my deputy, Paul Cramer. I suppose you know what we're here for."

"Scott just now told us."

"Well, let's get it over with. Where can I find these varmints?"

Scott scratched his three day growth of whiskers. "I don't rightly know. We just got back in town ourselves about two hours ago. They usually hang out at the Pearly Gate Saloon which you passed on your way in, but it might be a good idea to find out for sure if they're in there."

"How you going to do that?"

"Marshal, you two stay here with Jake while Billy and I mosey over to see my friend, Doc Carver. He's a frequent patron of the saloon and his going in there to buy a bottle of whiskey won't be anything out of the ordinary. When he steps out, he'll signal to me if they're there. Then we can work out our strategy."

"Don't worry about no strategy. If they're in there, we'll just go in and take 'em."

"Marshal, I'm not telling you how to do your job. You probably been doing pretty good for a long time without any help from me, but I'm gonna say this anyway. Those two hombres are real skittish, especially that dimwit called Marv, and they have a tendency to unholster their guns at the slightest provocation."

"I've handled their type before," McCabe said, patting his sawed off shotgun.

"That's just my point, Marshal. I know the poster says 'Dead or Alive,' but we want this feller alive. Remember? What I'm saying is, you two parade in their flashing your badges and I guarantee you there's going to be shooting before you clear the door."

"So, what do you suggest?"

"How about you two put those badges in your pocket and go in for a drink like you're just passing through. After a few minutes, Billy, Jake and I will come and take a table so they're between you and us."

"Go on," McCabe said.

"Now that's going to present a real problem for those yahoos, because, you see, my cousin here is half Navajo. Right before I went to Santa Fe, those two tried to run him out of town, but they had a sudden change of heart when I rammed a loaded Winchester in the back of Snake's head."

McCabe nodded. "I see. So you're figuring on diverting their attention to give Paul and me the opportunity to take them from behind. Is that it?"

"Yes sir, I believe that sums it up."

"What if they aren't there?"

Scott cast a sidelong glance at Billy. "Then Billy, here, becomes the sacrificial lamb. You know, when you want to kill the coyote or wolf that's running off with your sheep, you tie a lamb to a stake and you wait. The poor little thing bawls for his mama which attracts the coyote, and when he shows up, you got him."

Billy cleared his throat. "Excuse me, cousin, my name is Bear Heart, not Coyote Bait. I have a better idea. Suppose I go to the saloon and leave word with the bartender that you'll be waiting for Snake in front of the Pearly Gate at three o'clock this afternoon."

Scott grinned and took off for Doc's house. "It was just a thought. I'm on my way to Doc's"

•　　•　　•　　•　　•

Scott returned from Doc's house in less than ten minutes. Five minutes later Doc ambled across the deserted street and disappeared inside the Pearly Gate. It seemed like forever before Doc walked out with a bottle of whiskey in his hand. He paused to take off his hat and wipe his brow with his bandana before returning to his office.

"That's it." Scott said. "That's the signal. The coyotes are in there."

McCabe and his deputy removed their badges, mounted their horses and rode in silence to the Pearly Gate. After they dismounted, McCabe wrapped his sawed-off shotgun in his coat and moseyed toward the door. They pushed through the swinging doors and made straight for the bar, looking neither right nor left.

"Good afternoon, gentlemen," MacPhearson said. "Don't recall ever seeing you in here before. First time in Whiskey River?"

"Just passing through," McCabe replied amicably as he deposited his coat on the bar, "and stopped for something to wash the sand out of our craw. Two whiskies and some water to chase it with."

MacPhearson placed two glasses and a bottle of whiskey on the bar. While he went for the water, the two lawmen studied the patrons in the large mirror behind the bar. McCabe whispered to Cramer. "Which one you reckon is Snake?"

"The one with his chair tilted against the wall. Look at those eyes . . . real mean. Probably how he got his nickname. The other one doesn't look like he's got the sense to piss downwind."

As soon as MacPhearson returned with the water, Scott, Jake and Billy showed up at the door. Jake pushed the batwing doors open and paused to study the layout. McCabe and Cramer were straight ahead standing at the bar, their eyes glued on the mirror. Snake and Marv sat at a table to his left. Jake motioned for Scott and Billy to follow him to a table to the left of the two gunmen, placing them between the marshal and themselves.

They had no sooner taken their seats, when Snake brought his chair down on all four legs with a thud and stared at Scott. "Stable boy, I told you before, we got rules about Injuns in this here town. You got five seconds for you and that half-breed to clear out of here."

Scott held out his arms to show he wasn't armed. "And if I don't? What are you going to do, shoot an unarmed man?"

"No, I'm going to shoot an unarmed redskin. Ain't no law against that. No one's going to cry over a dead Injun."

Snake drew his pistol and pointed it a Billy. "You . . . outta here . . . now!"

Snake thumbed back the hammer. "You got 'til the count of

five. One . . ."

No one noticed the two strangers ease away from the bar. All eyes were glued on the pistol in Snake's hand and no one saw McCabe remove the sawed-off shotgun from his coat.

"Two . . ."

"Put the gun down," a quiet voice behind Snake commanded, accompanied by a loud click when McCabe cocked the shotgun. "I got a shotgun leveled at the base of your skull. If you think you're fast enough to wheel around and shoot me before I squeeze this trigger, you're welcome to try it. You're under arrest for the shooting of a deputy in Silver City and for conspiring to murder Jesse Chandler."

"That's bullshit. I ain't never been in Silver City and I shot Jesse Chandler in self-defense when he went for his gun."

Billy stared impassively at Snake as his eyes darted wildly from Marv to Billy. Marv licked his dry lips and edged away from Snake, his eyes fixed on McCabe and his shotgun. Out of the corner of his eye, Cramer, his pistol already in his hand, saw Marv go for his six-shooter and fired two shots at him. Cramer's bullets sent Marv sprawling to the floor, with a red splotch spreading on the front of his shirt.

Marv's lips moved and Cramer dropped to one knee to hear what he was trying to say. The hired gun managed a few words, loud enough for everyone to hear, "Hardin paid us five-hundred dollars to shoot Chandler and make it look like . . ." then closed his eyes as he struggled for breath.

"He's a lying sonnuva bitch," Snake screamed, his pistol still pointed at Billy.

Marv's eyes flickered open as he raised his gun in Snake's direction and fired one last shot. The bullet tore in to Snake's chest causing his gun to discharge. Marv managed a weak smile as he watched Snake sink to the floor. "You always thought you were the best, but deep down I knew I was faster than you, Snake," he said as his head flopped to one side and his eyes rolled back in his head.

"He may have been faster," Cramer said, "but he's also deader."

McCabe kicked Snake's gun away and rolled him over with the toe of his boot. "Don't know about this one."

A low moan came from where Jake was sitting. Billy lay slumped on the table with blood oozing from his right temple. "Somebody get Doc Carver," Jake yelled.

At that same moment Doc came busting through the door, his black bag in his hand. "When Scott told me what was up, I figured there'd be shooting."

"Doc, over here," Jake yelled, "Screw those two bungholes."

Doc bent over Billy and examined the wound. He removed the headband and said, "It's a damn good thing he was wearing this. Otherwise, he wouldn't have been so lucky."

"Yeah, some luck," Scott muttered.

"As far as I can tell, the bullet grazed his temple. Looks a lot worse than it is. Head wounds are like that. Here, Jake, hold this bandage real tight on the wound until it stops bleeding while I take a look at the other ones."

"I believe this is the only one that needs looking at, Doc." McCabe said.

Doc felt for a pulse then ripped off Snake's blood soaked shirt and found where the bullet had entered his right pectoral muscle and exited under his right armpit. "Looks like this one's going to live once we stop the bleeding, but he's going to be one aching sonnuva bitch. From the direction the bullet entered it should have torn through his shoulder, but apparently it was deflected downward by the collar bone, which I suspect might be broken."

"I ain't much interested in all them medical details, Doc," McCabe growled. "All I want to know is when is he going to be able to travel?"

"Other than the fact that he's going to hurt like hell, I'd say by tomorrow. I'll bandage him up good and after a night's rest to make sure the bleedings stopped, you can take him all the way to hell, if you want."

"I'm sure the devil's already rubbing his hands in anticipation," McCabe said, "but we need a place to lock him up tonight."

Cramer shot a glance at MacPhearson. "How about it bartender. You got a couple of rooms where we can stay and someplace to lock up this worthless chunk of cow dung?"

"I got a storeroom you can lock him in, but I won't be responsible for him. There are a couple of rooms upstairs you two can have."

Billy moaned and all eyes shifted to where he was now leaning back in his chair with Jake still pressing the bandage against his temple.

"I'm sorry Billy," Scott said. "I didn't mean to get you involved in this. Doc says you're going to be OK."

Billy put his hand to his head and murmured, "Aren't you supposed to shoot the coyote before it gets the lamb?"

Chapter Twenty-Seven

Sarah groaned and put her hand to her head. She winced as her fingers traced the lump on her forehead. She lifted her head and opened her eyes only to find herself staring into the fuzzy image of a face. Sarah blinked several times in an effort to bring it into focus, but the face remained anonymous. "What happened . . . where am I . . . who are you?" she said and let her head fall back with her eyes closed.

"You fell from your horse and hit your head. That's quite a nasty lump."

Fall? How did I fall? Lightning .That's it, lightning. Scared my horse. I suppose that's when I fell. Must have lost consciousness. How long have I been out? Am I dreaming, or is there really someone there? I'm so cold and my head hurts. Who is this man? Am I dreaming, or is there really someone there? I'm so cold and my head hurts.

Hardin knelt beside her and lifted her to a sitting position. He helped her slip into his coat and said softly, "Sarah, Sarah darling, wake up."

That voice! I know that voice.

Sarah's eyes fluttered open.

"It's me, Sam, Sam Hardin."

Sarah studied the face bending over her. *Sam Hardin? Seems familiar, but . . .*

Sarah shook her head. "I'm sorry. You seem to know me . . . at least you know my name, but . . ."

Before she could continue, Hardin said, "No matter. We've got to get you out of here. There's a line shack nearby, but we're going to have to ride double. Your horse must have spooked and run off."

Hardin helped Sarah mount, and then climbed aboard behind her. The rain continued to fall heavily as they headed for the shack where he and Sarah used to rendezvous. Sam had fixed it up better than the other line shacks, and made it clear to the outriders it was for his personal use only. Throughout all the years of Sarah's absence, Hardin kept it in immaculate condition in anticipation of the day Sarah would come back to him. It wasn't unusual for Hardin, in a fit of nostalgia, to ride to the shack and spend the afternoon holding a shawl and a pair of riding gloves that Sarah had left there on their last encounter . . . reminders of the warmth of her body and the softness of her hands.

Arriving at the shack, Hardin dismounted and carried Sarah inside where he gently placed her on a small sofa facing the fireplace. The light from a kerosene lantern fell on a shawl draped over the back of the sofa and a pair of riding gloves on the cushion next to her. She tried to make the connection, but nothing clicked. It was like a dream in which she knew all the answers, but was driven to frustration when she couldn't come up with them.

Whose are those?

Seems like I've seen them before.

Are they mine?

It they are, it means I've been here before, but I don't remember.

If they are mine, what are they doing here?

Hardin observed Sarah staring at the shawl and gloves. He picked them up and handed them to her. "Remember these? You left them here fifteen years ago. I knew you'd be back, so I've kept them for you all this time."

Sarah took the shawl and stared at the gloves. "No I don't remember ever being here."

"Well, it's a lot different now. I've fixed the place up, got rid of all the old furniture and spruced it up a bit. Come morning you'll recognize it in the light."

Sarah handed him back the shawl and gloves and said, "I can't make sense of anything right now. My head is spinning like a whirligig."

Hardin got a fire going and said, "Once you get out of those wet clothes and rest a bit, you'll be all right."

He took a clean nightshirt from an armoire next to the bed and handed it to Sarah. "Undress and put this on so I can hang them in front of the fire to dry."

Sarah gave Sam a dubious look and clutched his wet coat tighter around her.

That voice. I wish I could place that voice . . . and the face . . . it's like I should know who he is, but damn, why can't I remember? What is it? Something's telling me not to trust this man, but why?

Sam pulled a blanket off the bed and handed it to her along with a towel. "Here you can drape this over you. Don't worry. I won't peek."

Sarah took the blanket, draped it over her shoulders and turned away from Sam. After drying herself with the towel, she clutched the blanket tightly around her body and handed him her wet clothes. While he hung them on the back of a chair, she slipped into the nightshirt, and once again wrapped tightly in the blanket, returned to the sofa.

"Now it's my turn, except I won't need the blanket," Sam with a twisted smile. He undressed and put on dry clothes he took from the armoire, while Sarah stared blankly into the fire, her head somewhere in a distant world.

He hung his own wet clothes alongside Sarah's and settled on the sofa next to her with a bottle of MacPhearson's finest whiskey and two glasses. "Just like old times," he thought, envisioning their clothes strewn about as they tore at them in their eagerness to satisfy their passion. He poured out three fingers of the amber liquid and offered it to Sarah. "Here, drink this."

Without taking her eyes from the fire, she shook her head. *I'm so sleepy and my head hurts. Can't stay awake. Mustn't fall asleep. Can't help it . . . can't keep my eyes . . .*

Hardin held it in front of her. "Just a sip. Like the cowpunchers say, to kill the chill."

When Sarah made no reply, he downed it in one gulp and rested his head on the back of the sofa. "No wonder the Indians call it fire water," Hardin thought, as the whiskey seared his throat on its way to his belly. He leaned forward and poured himself another one. He raised the glass in Sarah's direction. "Here's to us, Sarah. I always knew you'd come back to me."

Sam reached out to pull her close, but Sarah was immobile. He prodded her gently, but she was unresponsive to his attempts to wake her. Hardin tossed back the whiskey and banged the glass on the table. He grabbed her shoulders with both hands and shook her roughly, "Wake up, damn it."

Sarah's head lolled from side to side, but her eyes remained closed. Hardin slapped her face. Sarah winced and uttered a soft moan, but, as if drugged, remained in a stupor. Hardin's euphoria brought on by the alcohol and the vision of Sarah's naked body snuggled against him dissolved into frustration. He reached down and snatched the blanket off her and stared lasciviously at her legs. He knelt before her and slipped his hands under the nightshirt and drew her close. His breathing became heavier as he caressed her body and whispered her name over and over in her ear. Sarah, drifting away, felt nothing.

Hardin rose and whispered. "I can wait. You sleep while I go back to the ranch for a few things. By morning you'll feel better and it'll be just like old times, you'll see."

•   •   •   •   •

Doc Carver bound up Snake's wound, leaving his right arm immobilized and helped Marshal McCabe move him to the storeroom. Snake groaned when McCabe pulled up two chairs and sat facing him.

McCabe pinned his badge to his vest and said, "My name is Joshua McCabe, but you can call me whatever the hell you like, because your sorry ass will soon be dangling from a rope. I'm the U.S. Marshal for the Territory of New Mexico and this here is my deputy, Paul Cramer. Now that we've gotten to know each other so well, I thought we ought to have a little chat."

He removed a paper from his shirt pocket, unfolded the "Wanted" poster and waved it in Snake's face.

Snake stared at it for a long time, then glared at McCabe. "I got nothing to talk about. Besides you got nothing on me. That thing in Silver City took place twenty years ago."

McCabe folded it up and put it back in his shirt pocket. "Well, that's where you're wrong, gunslinger. If you're referring to the statute of limitations, I got news for you. I did some checking. The deputy died six months after you hauled freight out of Silver City. Word is, it was your bullet that done him in."

"How do I know you're not making that up?"

The marshal patted his breast pocket. "Because I got a telegraph message right here from the sheriff of Silver City that says I'm not, and if I have to take you back there to prove it, by God, I'll do it."

Snake squirmed in the chair and grimaced. "I'm hurting real bad. You think I could get a drink of whiskey to ease the pain?"

McCabe said to his deputy, "Go get a bottle of painkiller from the bartender."

The marshal and his prisoner just stared at each other until

Cramer returned with the whisky. McCabe took the bottle, jerked the cork out with his teeth and filled the glass Cramer handed him.

Snake reached for it as far as the chain on the manacle would permit, but McCabe pulled it back. He spit the cork on the floor and said, "Not until we finish our little chat."

"For God's sake, man, this shoulder's killing me. Gimme the whiskey."

"The sooner we get this over with, the quicker you get the whiskey. It's up to you."

Snake groaned and has chin dropped to his chest.

McCabe took a sip, smacked his lips and said, "Hmm, that's mighty good stuff."

Snake's response was someplace between a moan and a whimper.

"Now here's the deal, hotshot," McCabe went on, "I take you back to Silver City and you're going to swing from a rope, but it doesn't have to be that way. You tell me what I want to know and I might look the other way on the other charge against you."

Snake's head snapped up. "What other charge you talkin' about?"

McCabe savored another sip of the whiskey. "In legal terms

it's conspiracy to commit murder. In plain talk, you took money to kill someone."

"What the hell you talking about? Took money to kill who?"

"Jesse Chandler, that's who. Sam Hardin paid you five hundred dollars to send him to boot hill."

"Wait a goddam minute," Snake yelled, "I shot the sonnuva bitch in self-defense. There were witnesses. They'll all tell you."

McCabe gave Snake a smug look. "Oh there were witnesses, all right. Like the one who overheard you and Sam Hardin when he paid you off for shooting Chandler. And there are witnesses who saw your partner plant the Derringer on Chandler. You shot an unarmed man because someone paid you to do it."

"That's bullshit." Snake screamed. "If Marv was here, he'd tell you."

"He already did . . . right before he cashed in his chips. A dying man's confession carries a lot of weight in a courtroom."

Snake shook his head. "No, no, Marv did that just to spite me. That dumb sonnuva bitch always fancied himself the fastest gun west of the Mississippi, but plain and simple, he was jealous of me."

McCabe shook his head. "It didn't have anything to do with you. He knew he was dying and just wanted to make his peace. But either way, you're between a grizzly bear and a cliff. I can haul you back to Silver City where they'll measure you for a wooden overcoat, or you'll do twenty years in prison for conspiracy. Unless. . ."

"Unless what?"

"Unless you testify against Sam Hardin, and maybe get off with just five years in the calaboose for cooperating with the prosecution."

"Go to hell," Snake snarled. "I'd rather do fifty years in prison than cooperate with you."

"Think about it gunslinger. All the people in prison whose friends and relatives you shot. Bad Snake Weston that everybody wants a piece of with a bum arm."

McCabe jabbed Snake in the shoulder and said, "Think about that."

Snake screamed in agony and jerked hard against the manacle on his left wrist.

Holding out the whiskey, McCabe said, "Here. You want this?"

Snake whimpered and reached for the whiskey, but McCabe threw it in his face. "You got all night to think it over. Tomorrow morning we ride for Silver City."

Chapter Twenty-Eight

Jake, Billy, and Scott waited until McCabe and his deputy disappeared into the storeroom with their prisoner before making their way to the door. As soon as they stepped outside, lightning crackled, followed by a thunderous boom in advance of a solid wall of water advancing inexorably toward them from the north end of town.

"We better get moving," Jake said as he slammed his hat on tight and bolted from the from the livery. All three reached the stable at the same time as a riderless horse, blowing hard, with its saddle hanging off to one side.

Scott grabbed the reins and led it inside the building. He studied the winded animal then spun around to ask Billy a question. "This morning, didn't Laura say she saddled the mare for Sarah?"

Billy nodded. "I believe that's what she said."

"She must have been in a hurry. Look how loose the cinch is, but the question is, where in the hell is Sarah?"

Jake scratched the back of his neck. "I don't like the looks of this. Something must have happened for this horse to show up winded like this. If Sarah had simply fallen off there's no way in God's creation this horse would have left her. Like all cow ponies, she's trained to stay put when the reins are hanging. No sir, something spooked this horse and Sarah could be lying out somewhere in this weather."

Jake lifted the left stirrup and slipped his fingers between the cinch and horse's belly. "Scott, why don't you run up to the house and fetch Laura."

Billy strode to the door and peered into the unrelenting downpour. "Hell of a time to be out there alone and on foot."

Minutes later Scott, accompanied by Teresa and Laura, came busting through the door. The two women shook out their slickers and walked over to the mare. Laura scratched the horse's ears and patted her neck before examining the cinch. "This has been tampered with. I always use two hitches, the first one on the saddle ring and a second one on the cinch ring. There's no second hitch and the first one is loose. Something or someone shooed her away."

Scott and Laura locked eyes. "OK, Laura, let's go on the assumption something spooked the horse. What . . . a cougar . . . a pack of coyotes . . . a rattlesnake?"

Billy shook his head. "Not likely. Animals aren't out on the prowl in a storm like this. More'n likely they'd be taking shelter."

Scott nodded. "So, if it didn't come loose on its own, it means someone loosened it, but who . . . and why?"

"To make it look like Sarah had an accident," was Laura's terse reply.

"Who would want to do that?" Teresa asked.

The thought of Sam Hardin holding his mother sent waves of fury through Scott's body. All of his scheming to trap Hardin and his love of the law went flying out the barn door. Billy was right. When you come right down to it, there's only one meaningful justice in the West, and Sam Hardin was about to get a good dose of it. He jerked his saddle and blanket off the rail and threw them on the Appaloosa. "Just one scoundrel I can think of, and I'm going after him right now," he said.

"Whoa, just a minute," Jake said before he could tighten the cinch. "We're not sure it was Hardin. Hell, just about everybody stands to lose something if Sarah boots him off her land. We got to make sure before we do something foolish."

"Who else could it be?" Scott replied. "It couldn't have been Snake or Marv, because they've been here all day. So get out of my way."

"I don't blame you for being riled, but what about all those people who got land from Hardin?" Teresa said. "Mrs. Gladstone, Mrs. Perkins, and Mrs. Avery were particularly hostile to Sarah when she and I went to the Emporium, and I'm betting the rest of those wives aren't too happy at the prospect of losing their homes either."

"That might be true, but I agree with Scott," Laura cut in. "As far as I'm concerned, there are only three people I know of here capable of doing such a thing, and two of them are accounted for."

Scott's eyes narrowed. "If he's capable of hiring Snake to kill Jesse, I wouldn't put it past him to do the same thing to Sarah and I got to get to him before he does."

"Oh, I don't think he would . . ."

Teresa caught Laura's eye before she could continue and signaled for her to keep quiet.

"Would what?" Scott asked.

"Nothing. As much I hate that pig, I just don't think he'd harm Sarah. At the same time I think we ought to have a plan before we just ride all over the countryside looking for her."

Scott yanked a slicker from a peg and said, "Well then, let's go back to the saloon and see what Snake knows about Hardin's whereabouts today."

•　　•　　•　　•　　•

The rain had slowed to a drizzle when Billy and Scott returned to the Pearly Gate. Scott checked the bowie knife in his waistband under the back of his vest, and pushed through the batwing doors. Just inside the door he called to MacPhearson, "Where's the marshal?"

"He went to fetch Doc."

"What's wrong? Something happen to Snake?"

"He didn't say, but you can ask him yourself. Here they come now."

"Howdy Marshal. Just came by to ask Snake a couple of questions. Is he all right?"

"He's OK. I guess I jabbed him a little too hard in the chest and I want to make sure he didn't spring a leak. What kind of questions you want to ask him?"

"About the time we got back to the livery, the horse Sarah Chandler rode out of town on this morning showed up minus Mrs. Chandler. The saddle cinch looks like it's been tampered with and we believe she's the victim of foul play. Since Sam Hardin is the only person who would greatly benefit from any harm coming to her, I just want to ask Snake what he knows about his boss's whereabouts today. That's all."

Doc Carver cleared his throat. "I believe I can save you the trouble. From where I sit at my desk, I have a clear view of the trails leading out of that end of town. When I saw Sarah ride out of town, I watched her until she was out of sight. I was about to turn back to what I was doing when I saw Sam Hardin come out from the alley behind Henderson's store and head in the same direction as Sarah."

"Why didn't you say something sooner?"

"Didn't think nothing of it. He didn't seem to be in any hurry, like he was following somebody. Hell, that's the route he usually takes when he's headed for his place, but now that you mentioned that thing about Sarah's horse, I would suspect that he was following her. If I were you, I'd be concerned."

"Well, I am concerned, and I'm riding out there right now to find out what's going on." Scott declared.

McCabe smoothed his walrus mustache before he spoke. "Whoa, just a minute, young feller. I don't want no vigilante justice going on here. I want everything legal like, so I'm sending the Deputy with you, just to make sure."

"Fine by me," Scott snapped, "but he better be ready to ride in ten minutes."

"Hold your horses. I reckon we better be thinking about how we're going to deal with Hardin," Cramer interrupted. "Sarah Chandler is his ace in the hole. If he's got her stashed away somewhere and we march right up and tell him Culpepper snitched on him, you can bet that's the last we're ever going to see of her."

"So, what are you saying, Deputy?" Jake asked.

"We tell him she's missing and we're out looking for her. We ask him if he might have seen her, and see where it goes from there, but we don't say a thing about what happened this afternoon. If he finds out Culpepper is dead and we got Snake, he just might hightail it outta here."

"So, who's gonna do the talking?" Scott asked.

Without hesitation Cramer said, "Jake Hardin might be more comfortable with that."

"OK," Scott agreed, "but what if he isn't there?"

"I don't even want to think about," Jake said, "I don't like the idea of Sarah alone with that skunk, but it's a damn sight better than wandering around out there alone."

"Well you better think about it," Billy said, "because finding her out there at night won't be easy. We have no idea where she was headed, and the rain has most certainly washed away her sign."

Chapter Twenty-Nine

By the time Sam Hardin reached the Lazy-H, the rain had stopped and the sky, a splash of gold, orange, and purple hues, was clearing, a prelude to the rapidly approaching darkness. There was no need for stealth . . . at this time of day the hands were either in the bunkhouse or off in town trying to run their dollar-a-day wages into a bonanza at the poker table. He dismounted and led his horse into the stable where he removed the saddle and placed it on a fresh mount.

Once inside the large, rambling house he exchanged his wet clothes for dry ones before rummaging in the kitchen for a few things to take back to the line shack. He placed the items in a clean flour sack and headed for the door. With his hand on the knob he hesitated, then went into the dining room where he removed a bottle of red wine from the sideboard. He didn't remember where he had gotten it, but he did recall putting it up for a special occasion, and Sarah's coming back to him was as special as it could get.

He was halfway back to the kitchen when the sound of approaching horses caught his attention. He put the wine down and lit a kerosene lantern. With his pistol in the other hand he stepped onto the front porch with the lantern held high.

"Who's there?" he called out as four riders approached.

"Jake Morgan here, with some friends."

Hardin held the lantern higher as they drew closer. "What you are doing out here this time of the night, Jake, and who's that with you?"

"You know Scott and his friend, Billy."

Jake nodded to his left and added, "And this here is Paul Cramer, Deputy Marshal from Santa Fe."

Hardin's eyes narrowed at the mention of Cramer. He nodded curtly and said, "You still haven't told me what you're here for, or why you brought the deputy with you."

"We're looking for Sarah Chandler. She rode out of town this morning and her horse showed up at the livery a couple of hours ago without her. We figured she might have taken shelter from the storm somewhere and we're just checking around."

Hardin shook his head. "Sorry to hear that, but I haven't seen her."

Scott leaned forward in his saddle. "Folks in town say they saw you come out of the alley behind Henderson's place and follow her."

Hardin bristled. "I don't give a damn what they say. I'm telling you I don't know where she is. Besides, why the hell would Sarah Chandler want to come here?"

Jake cut in quickly, "Scott, let me handle this."

"Look, Sam, nobody's saying she wanted to come here. Maybe she was just looking for a place to wait out the storm and wandered in here."

"Well, I already told you she ain't here, so you can pack up and leave."

Scott shrugged. "Why should I believe you?"

"What reason would I have to lie about it?"

Jake scowled at Scott and said, "Look, he said she isn't here. Now let's just go look someplace else for her."

"Sure, he'd say that. With her out of the way, there's no one to dispute his claim to the land. That's why."

"You really think I'd do something like that?" Hardin asked in mock surprise.

Scott shot right back, "If you paid Snake and Marv to kill her husband, what would stop you from killing his widow?"

Jake made a helpless gesture and shook his head in resignation.

"That's a damn lie." Hardin shouted.

"Is it?" Scott asked. "You offered me five hundred dollars to kill your two hired guns."

"That's another damned lie," Hardin yelled. "You can't prove any of that!"

"No, it's not. You know it and I know it, and I'm going to get you, Sam Hardin."

"I'll tell you what you can get. You can get off my property . . . right now!"

"Now, that's another mistake you just made," Scott continued in a taunting voice, "according to the information I just got in Santa Fe, this property is still in the name of Sarah Martinez Chandler, and you are trespassing. You know that and that's why I believe you know what happened to Sarah and where she is."

"That's bullshit. I filed a claim to this land based on what Jesse Chandler owed me. It's just a matter of time before the record is set straight."

Scott shook his head. "No, Sam, that claim won't hold water. You see, the property was never in Jesse Chandler's name. Even if he pledged the property against what he owed you, of which you have no proof, it wasn't his property to pledge."

Hardin sneered. "That's just a lot of palaver. We'll let the court decide that, and until they do, you can just ride out of here."

Paul Cramer, an interested onlooker up until that point, spoke up. "OK, Scott, that's enough. Let me handle it from here. Mr. Hardin, I can't force you to let us look around your place, but if you have nothing to hide, why not let us poke around a bit?"

Hardin was about to agree, but he suddenly remembered the sack of vittles and the bottle of wine sitting by the door and his horse all saddled up in the stable.

"All of you, get the hell off my land. I know my rights. You want to poke around, you get an order from a judge. Now git!"

Cramer turned to the other three. "I'm sorry, but that's what the law says, and it's my job to uphold the law. There's nothing more we can do here. Let's mosey."

At the front gate Scott fumed. "The sonnuva bitch is lying. He knows where she is or at least what happened to her. I got a notion to sneak back and take a look."

Cramer took Scott by the arm "You go back there and he spots you, he's got every right to plug you. Especially after the threats you just made. On the other hand, you shoot him, I got no choice but to arrest you. Now let's go back to town."

•　　•　　•　　•　　•

When the search party had left, Hardin scurried to the barn and tied the flour sack to the pommel of the saddle before pulling himself aboard his fresh mount. He emerged from the stable and was immediately bathed in the silvery glow of a full moon. He pulled the horse back into the shadow of the building and headed for the tree-lined path to the main gate, darkened by the shadows of the sycamores and aspens. The rain softened ground muffled the cadence of the horse's hooves as it cantered toward the arch with the large Lazy-H chiseled out of a single pine board. Once he was safely out of earshot, he put his spurs to the horse's flanks and road at a reckless gallop toward his long awaited reunion with his "beloved Sarah." Giddy with anticipation, he didn't observe the shadowy figure slip from the brush and fall in behind.

·   ·   ·   ·   ·

With the storm well to the south of Whiskey River, the bright moon lit their way, as they rode in silence . . . Jake in the lead, followed by Scott and Cramer, with Billy bringing up the rear. After a while Scott pulled even with Jake and recounted in detail his visit to the Mission. Jake listened intently, nodding his understanding every now and then. He only showed surprise at the revelation that Billy was kin to Sarah.

"That's right, Jake, Don Lucas Fernando Martinez is Billy's father, which makes him a cousin of sort to me."

"Well, I'll be. All the while I thought you were just smarting off about him being your cousin, and it turns out he really is. Not only that, but what does it make him to Sarah, and what kind of claim could he have to the land?"

"Good questions, Jake. I'm going to have to look into that."

"On the other hand," Jake pondered aloud, "how do we know the story this Rosario told you ain't just some concoction of hers?"

Scott nodded. "There is that possibility, but somehow, I feel she's telling the truth. Besides she's got the old feller's family bible with all the family history recorded in it."

Jake muttered something to himself and once again fell silent.

Cramer was content to keep his thoughts to himself and figured Billy wanted to likewise, and that's how they rode until Jake and Scott pulled up at the railroad tracks and waited for the other two to catch up. About a minute later, only Cramer showed up.

"Where's Billy?" Jake asked.

Cramer turned in his saddle and stared in disbelief. "He was right behind me, leastways I thought he was."

"Hey Billy," Scott called out. "Where the hell are you?"

The nocturnal chirping, croaking, and whistling came to an abrupt halt at the sound of Scott's voice. When there was no reply, Scott called out again. Ultimately, the gradual resumption of the cacophony of the creeping and crawling creatures of the night was the only response. "Ain't that just like a damn Injun," Cramer muttered, "they sneak away from you just as easily as they sneak up on you."

"He ain't no damn Injun," Scott growled, "he's my cousin."

Cramer shrugged. "Sorry, where do you suppose he got off to?"

"Knowing Billy, he's probably watching every move Hardin makes. Come daylight, we'll know a lot more than we know right now."

Cramer pointed a finger at Scott. "And I'm watching every move you make, so don't get any notion about slipping off and joining your cousin."

"Now why would I do a thing like that?" Scott said with an angelic look.

Chapter Thirty

Sarah awoke with a start, the throbbing in her head reduced to a dull ache. From her sitting position on the sofa she surveyed the room in the amber light of the dying fire, and then studied the garment she was wearing with a puzzled look.

How did I end up with this nightshirt? Where am I? How did I get here?

With an effort she got up and walked stiffly around the room stopping here and there to examine a chair, a candleholder, a lamp, the nightstand, and the bed. When these and other familiar objects teased her memory into recognition, she rolled her hands into fists and pounded the air.

Oh, my God! No wonder that voice was familiar. It was Sam Hardin, and this is . . . oh no, no, no! Only he would have brought me here.

She looked at herself in the nightshirt again and ripped it off. "That filthy bastard!" she muttered

Sarah, naked and shaking with rage, whirled at the sound of an approaching horse. She draped the blanket over her shoulders and jerked her clothes from the back of the chair. She bent over, scooped up her boots, and slipped out the back door, just as the horse pulled up in front of the cabin.

•   •   •   •   •

Sam Hardin dismounted and hurriedly looped the reins over the hitching rail. He loosened the flour sack from the saddle horn and quietly opened the door. "Sarah," he called softly, "Sarah, my love, I'm back."

He approached the sofa from the back and said, "Time to get up. I brought something to eat . . . and this." He held up the bottle of wine. "I've been saving it for this very day, the day you came back to me, like I always knew you would."

When there was no reply, he called out in a stern voice, "Sarah, wake up," and strode around to the other side. At the sight of the vacant sofa, he threw his head back and let out a yell that welled up from the very depths of his anguish. His long awaited dream, suddenly come true, had turned into a cruel joke. How much longer could Sarah torment him? But, Sam Hardin would not tolerate such an affront to his ego. He would not be denied his conquest. He had waited too long for this moment. Sarah would be his again! His twisted desire filled him with a morbid resolve to find her and force her to submit to him.

Hardin rushed out the front door and scanned the moonlit

terrain listening intently for any sound of Sarah. The silence was oppressive.

"Sarah," he bellowed, "where are you? Come back. You see, Sarah, this is the way it was meant to be. Just you and me. You always belonged to me. I can't let you go now. Don't you understand that? You are mine!"

·   ·   ·   ·   ·

In the heavy brush behind the shack about twenty paces from the outhouse, Sarah quaked with loathing for the man who would take advantage of her while she was unconscious. While Hardin ranted at the sky, she struggled into her clothes. The suede riding skirt blended with the reddish terrain, but in the brilliant moonlight, her white blouse was like a beacon. She decided she'd better hang on to the blanket.

Her mind worked frantically sorting out the possibilities. *He'd notice that my clothes are gone, so what would he assume? That I fled . . . or was hiding nearby? Would he take off looking for me, or would he wait until daylight? What about Laura and Teresa? Would they come looking for me? How would they know where I am?*

While these and other questions raced through her mind, the back door of the cabin flew open and Sam Hardin stood in the doorway peering into the clumps of sagebrush and cactus shimmering in the moonlight. Sarah, hunkered down behind a thicket, felt his eyes boring right through the blanket that she had pulled over herself, head and all. Hardin stepped over the threshold and took several steps in her direction before stopping to once again survey the silvery emptiness.

The pounding in Sarah's ears was so loud, she thought for sure he would hear it. When everything else screamed at her to get up and run, her survival instincts told her to stay. That and the memory of jackrabbits on the ranch how they hide in the brush blending in with their surroundings and not moving a muscle, until the danger had passed. The pressure in her chest was unbearable, but she willed herself to be a jackrabbit. All at once, Hardin veered off to his right toward the outhouse.

Hardin tapped on the door. "Sarah, are you in there?"

When there was no answer he jerked the door open and quickly slammed it shut. "You can't hide from me, Sarah. I know you're here, and when I find you . . ."

Sarah winced and bit her lip as her left leg started to cramp. The pain was unbearable . . . she had to stretch her leg. Little by little she straightened the leg, stopping at the slightest sound lest it give her away. It was almost fully extended when Hardin whirled suddenly and strode rapidly in her direction. Sarah heard the footsteps and covered mouth with her left hand to stifle a scream. It sounded like he was right on top of her. At that moment a jackrabbit bolted from a clump of sagebrush right below his feet, not more tan an arm's length from where Sarah lay in concealment.

Hardin raised his pistol and, out of sheer frustration, fired three shots at the fleeing animal. Sarah, unaware of what was going on, choked on the screams wadded in her throat. It wasn't until she heard Hardin yell, "Take that, you miserable creature," that she realized what had taken place.

She lay frozen, unsure if Hardin was still lurking nearby. She desperately wanted to take a peek, but she remembered the jackrabbit. She tried counting the seconds, anything to keep her mind off her precarious situation. She prayed, keeping track of the Hail Mary's on her fingers, but her mind, swathed in terror, kept wandering. Then she heard a door close. After what seemed like eons, she slowly, imperceptibly pulled the blanket back far enough to catch a glimpse of the cabin. The back door was closed. Hardin must have gone back inside.

Sarah was about to get up when the vision of a jackrabbit concealed in a bramble, loomed in her head. It would abandon its hiding place only when there was no longer any danger, or flight was the only other option. Flight at that moment was not an option for Sarah. She continued to study the scene from her temporary haven and drew her breath in sharply when she espied Sam Hardin leaning against the side of the cabin with his back to her. Every once in a while he would turn to check out the area where Sarah lay in hiding. The hours dragged by, but Hardin maintained his persistent vigil. With dawn imminent, it would only be a matter of time before she would be discovered. The time for flight had arrived. She raised herself to a crawling position and inched herself away from the cabin. With the blanket draped over her back, she looked like a huge terrapin with her eyes continually checking on Hardin. Every time he turned his head in her direction, she froze in her tracks. By daybreak she had put enough distance between the cabin and herself to stand up and run, but she thought," Where can I go where he won't find me?"

．　．　．　．　．

The next morning Scott woke up to find Billy stretched out on a blanket on the floor. He poked him in the ribs with is toe and asked, "Where the hell you been?

Billy sat up and yawned as he stretched his tired body. "Ain't used to sleeping on the ground. I'm getting soft. Like you palefaces."

"Go to hell. Where did you disappear to last night?"

"Thought I'd do some checking on Hardin. I doubled back and waited to see what he'd do."
"Why didn't you say something?"

"After the deputy's speech about upholding the law and what's legal and what's not, I figured it'd be better if I just took off on my own."

"So what did you see?"

"About ten minutes after I got there, he comes out the back door with a sack in his hand and heads for the stable. Pretty soon he comes out the stable with the sack tied to his saddle horn and rides out real sneaky like. It was easy following him for a while, but then clouds blocked out the moon and I lost him near some woods. I tried to find some sign, but it was too dark. As wet as the ground is I won't have any trouble picking up his trail in the daylight."

Scott pounded his fist. "That lying coyote does know where Sarah is. He's got her stashed away someplace."

"That would be my guess," Billy said as he pulled his moccasins on, "and the sooner we find her the better."

"And," Scott added with a wink, "there's no sense in bothering the Marshal with this, seeing how he's tied up with Mr. Snake, right?"

"Naw, all their legal shit would just get in the way of justice."

"Then it's settled. Let's ride."

"Ride where?" Laura asked as she backed into the room with a tray of coffee, biscuits and bacon.

Laura placed the tray on a small table and sat on the edge of the bed while Scott and Billy wolfed down the biscuits and bacon. When they were done, she asked again, "Where are you two fixing to ride to, and don't give me any cock and bull story."

Under her withering glare, Scott knew that anything but the truth would be useless. "Billy you tell her."

Laura folded her arms and said, "Tell me what?"

Billy drained the last of his coffee and cleared his throat. "OK, it's like this. After we left the Lazy-H last night, I doubled back to see what Hardin was up to. When I saw him ease out the kitchen door, I followed him."

Laura's expression changed from skeptical to interested. "What happened next?"

"Once he left his place, he put the spurs to his horse like he was going somewhere in one helluva hurry. It was easy following him in the moonlight until it clouded over and I lost him. Scott and I were heading to the spot where I lost sight of him to see if we could pick up his tracks."

"So that's where you're heading. Well not without me you're not, and I expect Jake and Teresa want to be in on this as well."

Scott massaged the back of neck. "Aw, Laura, too many folks

will just get in the way."

"Well that's just too bad. We have just as much as stake in this as you, so like it or not, we're all going together . . . and that includes Doc Carver."

"Why should all of us go rampaging all over the countryside when there's no assurance we'll find him," Scott argued in one last attempt to dissuade her.

Laura stood with her hands on her hips and allowed herself a smug smile. "You don't have to worry about that. I know where she is."

"Wait a minute," Scott countered, "how do you know where she is?"

"Maybe it's just woman's intuition or maybe it's something she said while we womenfolk were gabbing yesterday," Laura said suggested.

"But, Laura, it could be dangerous. There might be shooting."

Laura's coy smile turned into a steely glare. "If I have any say about it, I guarantee you there'll be shooting."

Scott looked helplessly at Billy.

Billy shrugged, "Let's ride."

Laura shook her head. "Not without Jake and Teresa. You two go up to the house and tell them while I go fetch Doc Carver just in case Sarah's hurt. We'll all meet here in fifteen minutes."

Laura picked up the tray with the remnants of breakfast and barked at Scott, "*Andale*, get moving. I'm going to pour the rest of this coffee down Doc's throat."

Chapter Thirty-One

"Doc . . . Doc Carver . . . For God's sake, wake up."

Doc, seated at his desk with his chin resting on his chest, partially opened one eye, mumbled something unintelligible, and resumed his rhythmic breathing.

Laura grabbed him by the lapels of his coat and shook him. "Dammit, Doc, wake up! Sarah's missing and we gotta find her. God knows what happened to her or where she is, now wake up."

Doc rubbed eyes, grimaced and reached for the whiskey bottle that had slipped from his hand when he drifted into dreamland. Laura snatched the empty bottle and poured him a cup of black coffee from the pot on the stove.

"Here, this is what you need . . . and some biscuits to go with it. Get yourself together while I hitch the horse to the buggy."

Doc knocked back two swallows of the tepid coffee and made a wry face. "You sure this isn't some of Jake's horse liniment? Now, what was that you were saying about Sarah?"

Halfway out the door Laura called back, "Just get your stuff together. I'll tell you on the way."

• • • • •

Jake saw Scott and Billy coming up the walk from the livery and met them on the front porch. "Well, Billy, I see you found your way back. You get lost?"

"No, I decided to double back and see if Hardin was up to anything. Sure enough, about a half hour after we left, he took off and I followed him until the moon clouded over. Then I lost him."

Jake nodded knowingly. "I knew it. I just plain knew it. That no good, lying sonnuva bitch knows where Sarah is. You think you could pick up his trail from where you last saw him?"

"No problem there, but Laura says that won't be necessary . . . says she knows where he's holed up with Sarah and as soon we're ready, she's gonna take us there, all of us."

Jake scratched the stubble of his chin. "How in the hell would she know that?"

Billy shook his head. "Don't rightly know. She said it was something Sarah mentioned when the womenfolk were having their pow wow yesterday."

Jake stuck his head in the door and called his wife. "Billy here says Laura told them she knows where Sarah is because Sarah mentioned it when you three were talking yesterday. Do you recall

Sarah saying anything about where she might be heading when she took off yesterday?"

Teresa shot a quick glance at Scott and shook her head. "I don't recall anything like that. Sarah only said she wanted to take a ride to clear head, but, you know Laura . . . once she gets a notion in head, there's no talking her out of it."

"You're right about that, but I tell you what, we're just wasting time bumping our gums over it. You get yourself ready and I'll hitch the team to the buckboard."

"Where's Laura now?"

"She went to fetch Doc Carver . . . probably had to sober him up, but I reckon she's used to that by now."

Teresa shook her head slowly as she undid her apron. "If it weren't for Laura, who knows what would become of Doc. Heaven only knows why she looks after him the way she does, like she's his guardian angel."

•　　•　　•　　•　　•

Sarah drew the heavy Indian blanket tightly around her, but she still felt the sting of the north wind that drove the storm through the previous day. Thirsty and hungry, her head throbbed with each step, but she dared not stop. Hardin would certainly pick up her tracks in the soft ground and she had to find help before he found her. The woods had become thicker and Sarah tried her best not to leave footprints by walking on the rocks and pine needles, but in her panic, she wasn't doing a very good job of it. Every now and then she would pull up behind a tree to listen, but all she heard was the heavy dew dripping from the trees. Hardin could be right behind her and she wouldn't know it. Sarah forced herself to press on and after another hour, she came to a place on the edge of the woods where the land had been cleared. She let out an audible sigh of relief when she spied a house about a hundred yards away at the far edge of the clearing. Apparently, not much had been done with the land since it was cleared . . . sagebrush, brambles, and cactus had taken over the spaces between the stumps, and there was no sign of activity.

Sarah's heart raced with hope, but she was too exhausted to continue. She ventured from the shelter of the trees and slumped on one of the stumps to get her breath before pushing on toward the house. The sun was higher in the sky and she shed the heavy blanket, but the fierce heat and lack and water caused her to grow faint. As she felt herself slipping away, a feeling of dread enveloped her.

Chapter Thirty-Two

Outside the livery Jake sat in the buckboard with Teresa at his side and his double barrel shotgun across his lap. Laura, with Doc Carver slouched at her side, swung the buggy in a half circle and brought it alongside the buckboard. Scott stepped out from the stable with his gun belt strapped to his waist and his Winchester in his hand. He slipped the rifle in the saddle holster and swung aboard the Appaloosa.

"Where in hell is Billy?" Jake asked.

"He said it might not be a good idea for all of us to take off at once. Could make the wrong people suspicious, so he left a while ago and will meet us outside of town," Scott replied.

Jake nodded. "Good idea. Laura, why don't you and Doc take off like you're going on a sick call and the three us will meet up with you along the way to the Lazy-H."

Laura shook the reins and the horse leaned into the traces. "By the way," Jake called after her, "how'd you figure out where Hardin might be?"

Before she could reply, Scott saw Teresa poke her in the ribs with her elbow and heard her say through tight lips, "Let it be, Jake."

"What was that, Jake?" Laura called over her shoulder.

"I just wanted to know . . ."

Teresa answered for him. "It's nothing. Get going."

Jake, with a puzzled look asked, "What the heck is going on? I was just curious about . . ."

Teresa motioned toward Scott with her eyes and whispered, "Just let it be Jake. Let them get out of sight across the track and then we'll take off."

Scott nudged his horse alongside the buckboard and asked, "Is there something I should know about?"

"Not especially," Teresa said with a bland look.

•　　•　　•　　•　　•

Sarah stared at what she hoped would be her refuge, but deep within her soul she knew there was something wrong with the picture laid out before her.

I must be going crazy with the heat. When I crawled away from the cabin, the sun was on my left, so I was heading south. But, now the sun is on my right . . . oh no, dear God no! I must have been walking in one big circle for the past few hours.

Sarah gave in to her despair and began to cry. The realization that the house on the edge of the clearing was Sam Hardin's line shack crushed her spirit. She drew the blanket tighter around her and sobbed uncontrollably. When the tears finally stopped, Sarah took stock of her situation.

From a distance I probably don't look any different from all the stumps scattered about. As long as I stay under this blanket, I guess I'm safe. But, I'll pass out from the heat. And . . . where is Hardin? I don't see any sign of him nor his horse. Maybe it's tied up on the other side, or maybe he's out looking for me. I can't stay out here any longer, especially without water. I'll burn up. I better get back into the woods.

Sarah got up and keeping low, made her way back to the safety of the trees. She stood in the shade of an ancient cottonwood, arched her back and breathed a deep sigh of relief, one that was short-lived. On the opposite side of the tree, Sam Hardin stood waiting for her.

Chapter Thirty-Three

When Billy got to the place where he last saw Hardin the night before, he dismounted and studied the ground.

"Do you see anything?" Scott asked.

"Lots of sign. Some coming and some going," Billy said from his squatting position.

"Damn," Scott said, "There's no way of telling if he's at the Lazy-H or wherever it is he was coming from. What do you think, Jake?"

Jake shook his head, "Beats me."

Laura was about to speak when Teresa caught her eye. "Laura, what makes you think you might know where Sarah is?"

Laura shrugged. "Nothing special. It's just that when Billy described the place where he lost Hardin last night, I remembered there were a couple of line shacks nearby, a good place to wait out a storm. I figured it might be a good idea to give them the once over."

Scott fixed her with a dubious look. "This morning you sounded emphatic. Now you're not so sure."

Laura flipped her hair back with a toss of her head. "Maybe I've had time to think it over, but I still think we should take a look."

"How far are they from here?" Jake asked.

"About a half hour I'd say. The one I'm thinking of is on the edge of some land he cleared, so it's not going to be easy to sneak up on the place, especially if we go busting in there like drunken cowhands on payday."

Billy intuited that Laura knew more than she was allowing, so he said to her, "Take the lead, since you know the way. Stop at the edge of the clearing and we'll decide how to take it from there. Is that all right with you folks?"

Everybody nodded in agreement and Jake and Teresa fell in behind the buggy while Scott and Billy broke off to the side keeping them in view.

●　　●　　●　　●　　●

Hardin's tone was solicitous. "Sarah, my love, what do you mean running off like that? You really had me worried."

Sarah stared blankly at him. "Worried? You? Who are you? What am I doing here?"

Hardin's eyes narrowed as he studied her closely. Sarah

maintained her composure under his intense scrutiny and returned the angry stare with the guileless innocence of a small child.

His face softened and he said in a kinder tone, "You're Sarah Chandler and you took a fall. You must still be suffering from the blow to your head. Let's go to my place over there where you can rest."

Sarah put her hand to the purple mark on her forehead and pulled it back instinctively.

"It's all right Sarah. You have nothing to worry about. I promise."

Sarah continued to look dubious.

"There's nothing to be afraid of. After you've had something to eat, I'll ride into town and get Doc Carver to come take a look at you."

Sarah knew he was lying, but the mention of food overcame her good sense. He took her by the arm and led her across the clearing to the cabin. Once inside he spun her around and held her tightly in his arms. "Sarah, my darling, you can't imagine how long I have waited for this moment, to have you back in my arms, to feel your body so close to mine."

He bent over to kiss her, but Sarah shook her head from side to side and pushed hard with both hands against his chest. Hardin held her tighter and with one hand grabbed her hair and forced her head to remain still while he pressed his mouth against hers. Sarah clamped her lips shut and struggled even harder.

Her resistance only excited him further. He kissed her neck, her cheeks and explored her ears with his tongue. He released her hair and placed both hands on her buttocks and pulled her back and forth in a rocking motion. She could feel the bulge pressing against her and the rage she had stifled all these many years erupted with a fury. Sarah pounded his chest with her fist and screamed for him to stop. Hardin roared with a savage delight. With one arm still holding her tightly against him, he grabbed the front of her blouse with the other and ripped it open exposing her bare breasts.

"Let me go, you maniac. For God's sake, let me go!"

Hardin buried his face in her cleavage. "Not now, my love. Not after all these years. I can't wait for us to make love again like we used to."

Sarah drew her face back and spat, "Never, you despicable pig."

Hardin's face contorted with rage and he slapped her hard across the face.

Sarah screamed, "Never, you hear me. Never, never." Hardin clamped his hand over mouth and with his face close to hers, he snarled, "Oh, yes. Now, and whenever I want. You see, you're mine Sarah. You belong to me. You better get used to it."

Sarah, now struggling for every breath, shook her head violently from side trying to free herself. Hardin removed his hand from her mouth and she took in deep, gasping breaths until little by little her normal color returned and she breathed more calmly. Then he pulled her head back by her hair and said, "There's no reason things can't be like they used to be. I know the only reason you left is because of Jesse, but he's gone. You loved me then and you can love me again."

Sarah steeled herself and said in an icy voice, " I remember, Sam. I remember that I never loved you. I was a frustrated housewife looking for some excitement and you just happened to be handy. I've hated myself all these years for being such an imbecile, and the thought of you touching me makes me want to vomit. And one more thing, I didn't come back to Whiskey River because of you. Get that through your arrogant, conceited head."

Hardin's nostrils flared and his eyes blazed a moment before he sent her sprawling with a backhand across her mouth. Sarah wiped at the trickle of blood that appeared at the corner of her mouth, her eyes locked in a defiant glare.

Chapter Thirty-Four

The trail, dotted with mesquite, cactus, and occasional cottonwood, snaked its way through the rolling terrain until it ended in a clearing with a cabin at the far side. Laura reined in the horse at the edge of the clearing and waited for the others to catch up. When they were all gathered alongside the buggy, Scott asked Laura, "Is that the place you were talking about?"

"It's one of them. There are a couple of others farther down the line."

Billy shaded his eyes and scanned the area surrounding the cabin. "Can't tell from here if anyone's in there or not," he said. "Of course his horse could be around the back. I could circle around and take a look."

Jake cocked his head to one side and said, "Don't think it's going to make any difference. We're going to have a helluva time sneaking up on that shack. This buckboard makes more noise than a cat in heat. Anybody got an idea?"

"How about this?" Laura said, "I don't think Hardin would

suspect anything if Doc and I were to drive up to the shack with Jake and Teresa tagging along. We're simply out looking for Sarah and asking around. What's he got to fear from Doc, Jake, and a couple of women?"

"What about Billy and me?" Scott asked.

"Look at the cabin," Laura said, "the only door or windows I see are in the front. There might be a back door or even a window, but on the side we can from here, I don't see any. If you two can work your way to the side of the house, there's no way he'll see you without exposing himself."

Billy and Scott eyed each other and nodded in unison and Laura continued, "All right, we'll wait until you two are in position then we'll just ride up like we got nothing to hide. What do you think, Doc?"

Doc scratched his chin whiskers while he thought it over. "I honestly believe Sam Hardin is a bit touched. If he's got Sarah in there with him and feels threatened by us, there's no telling what he'll do. Why don't you let me do the talking when we get there?"

Everyone nodded in agreement and Laura took it from there. "OK, you two get going. When we see you at the side of the shack, we'll move in."

Scott pulled up alongside the buggy and gave Laura's shoulder a squeeze. Their eyes met and he said, "Be careful. I don't want anything to happen to you."

Laura reached for his hand and replied, "You too. You're already my hero, so you don't have to prove it this morning."

•　　•　　•　　•　　•

Hardin grabbed Sarah by the arm and jerked her to her feet. He pulled her close holding her right arm behind her back and clutched a handful of hair with his left and forced her head back. He lowered his head to kiss her when a voice broke the silence.

"Sam Hardin. Are you there?"

Hardin released her hair and spun her around. He drew his pistol and held it against her temple. With his right arm around her neck he pulled her close using her as a shield. "Not a sound," he whispered as he pushed her toward the door and quietly slipped the barrel bolt in place.

"Sam, this is Doc Carver. If you're in there, open up. We need to talk to you."

Sarah took a deep breath and was about to scream when Hardin smashed her in the cheek with the butt of his gun. With the salty taste of her own blood in her mouth, Sarah realized if she didn't act at once, she might never get another chance. She drew her leg back and kicked Hardin in the shin with the side of her boot and screamed as she tried to spin out of his grasp.

When Laura heard the scream, Doc had to restrain her from jumping out of the buggy. "Hold on there, young lady, no sense in both of you getting hurt. Let me handle this."

Doc got down from the buggy and stood in front of the door. "Sam, this is Doc Carver. We know Sarah Chandler got thrown from her horse and we think she may have wandered this way in the storm. We just want to know that she's all right."

With his arm still around Sarah's neck, he slid back the bolt and opened the door a crack. "What makes you think she's here?"

"We just heard her cry out like she was hurt. I think I ought to come in and take a look at her."

Hardin opened the door just enough so Doc could see him holding the gun to Sarah's head. "You come busting in here, I'll kill her. I mean it. Now get the hell off my property."

"Now, Sam, be reasonable," Doc pleaded. "We don't want any trouble. You just let Sarah go, and we'll forget the whole thing."

"Who's out there with you?"

"Just Laura, Teresa and Jake. That's all. We come real peaceable like, Sam."

Hardin opened the door and stood in the doorway with the pistol still to Sarah's head. "How do I know there ain't somebody hiding around the corner of the house?"

Doc held out his hands. "I have no reason to lie to you, Sam. We just want to make sure Sarah's all right."

Hardin took two cautious steps forward and stopped, his eyes darting from side to side.

"Sam, I'm not armed. Now look here, you've got yourself into a fine mess. That U.S. Marshal and his deputy are still in town and if Sarah doesn't show up soon, they're fixing to take you in for kidnapping. If you'll let me, I believe I can help you. You just let Sarah go, and I can explain that I've been treating you for a nervous breakdown . . . that you're not responsible for your actions. Shucks, I got a feller off the same way back East. They were going to railroad him for killing a man who he said raped his wife. I convinced the jury he didn't know what he was doing . . . that he was out of his mind with grief. So put the gun down and let's work this thing out."

"Step aside you drunken fool. You think I can't see through that bullshit? Take one more step and I'll blow a hole in her head."

Doc put his arms up in surrender and moved off to Sam's left just as Scott stepped out from behind the cabin and approached Hardin with his Colt .45 hanging in his hand.

Hardin pressed the barrel of the gun tighter against Sarah's temple. "You hold it right there, you smart-alecky son-of-a-bitch, and stay out of this. This ain't none of your affair."

Scott chose his words carefully. "But this is my affair. You see my name isn't Scott Martin. It's Luke Chandler. You killed my father, but you're not going to kill my mother."

"Ain't that noble of you," Hardin sneered. "So this is your mother. Let me tell you about your dear, sweet mother. You ever wonder why she upped and left your pa? I'll tell you why."

"Don't listen to him," Sarah screamed. "He's . . . he's . . ."

Hardin tightened his grip around Sarah's neck and choked off the rest of the sentence. "He kicked her cheating ass out. Bet you didn't know she was stepping out on him, did you?"

Sarah struggled in vain to free herself, but Hardin's grip was unyielding.

"While your pa was working his butt off, she was screwing me all over the territory. You have no idea how many different places and how many different ways we did it. Now, what do you think of this tramp?"

Scott lifted his pistol and aimed it at Hardin's head. "Shut up! Shut up, you hear! Turn her loose or I'll put a bullet in your filthy mouth."

Hardin relaxed his hold on Sarah and she managed to cry out, "It wasn't like that, Luke . . ."

Hardin laughed as he choked off the rest of the sentence. "You ain't heard the best part. For two years I was cuckholding your old man and he didn't do shit about it. Instead of settling it like a man, after he kicked your ma out, for revenge he raped my Abigail and she and the child died in childbirth. So you see, Luke Chandler, I couldn't let him get away with that, but before I could settle his hash, Snake caught him cheating at cards and put a bullet in him."

Scott took careful aim at Hardin, but lowered the gun to wipe the tears from his eyes with his shirtsleeve.

Doc Carver broke the silence. "That's a damned lie, Sam. Jesse Chandler never cheated anybody. You paid Snake to shoot the wrong man."

Hardin's face, purple with rage, screamed, "That's not true. He raped my Abigail and now I'm finally going to get my revenge. A wife for a wife."

"I'm telling you, Sam, it wasn't rape and it wasn't Jesse."

"What do you mean it wasn't Jesse? How in the hell would you know, you drunken old fool?"

Doc's gravel voice belied his angelic look. "Because, when Abigail conceived, I was the only other one present. As much as it may pain you to hear this, I can assure you it wasn't rape."

"That's a damned lie. You're lying just to save Sarah. It had to be Jesse," Hardin snarled. "That was the only way a coward like him would get back at me."

"My father was no coward," Luke yelled as he raised his pistol again and took careful aim.

Sarah screamed, "Luke! No, Luke! He's . . ."

A single shot echoed across the clearing and Laura screamed as Sarah, spattered with blood, sagged to her knees.

Teresa bolted from the buckboard to cradle Sarah in her arms. Laura jumped from the buggy and raced to where Luke stood in a daze. She threw her arms around him and buried her face in his chest. "Thank God, it's over. I was so worried something awful was going to happen to you."

Luke lowered the pistol and with his free hand pulled Laura closer. He gawked at Doc holding a Derringer in his outstretched hand, then at Sam Hardin lying on the ground with blood gushing from a gaping hole in the left side of his head.

He shifted his gaze back to Doc who held out the Derringer. "There's some might say there's no justice out here. Law of the gun and all that bullshit, but there ain't a bit of truth in that. There is justice . . . although it takes a strange turn. Take this pistol, for instance . . . it's the one Marvin Culpepper planted on your father the night Snake shot him. I took it off him when I examined him lying there on the floor of the saloon. It's not unusual for gunfighters to carry a hide-away gun, so it didn't surprise me that

Marv would have a pistol like this. What did surprise me was what was engraved on the barrel. Take a gander at it. You'll notice it's got Hardin's name engraved on it. That should remove any doubt that Hardin put Snake up to it."

Scott took the Derringer and rubbed his fingertip over the engraving. "Snake shot by his own partner, and Hardin killed by his own gun. Yeah, Doc, I guess there is a strange kind of justice out here. But, does it make any sense that Hardin would leave something on the body that would incriminate him?"

"I often thought about that myself, but if neither Snake nor Marv owned one, where else were they going to get one? That was probably the only one in Whiskey River that any one knew of. Marv couldn't have bought one from the Emporium without the whole town knowing about it. So I figured, after Jesse was shot, he'd discover' it and just keep it. The problem is, he didn't kill Jesse, and I got to him before he had a chance to remove it."

Teresa helped Sarah to her feet and she stared incredulously at Doc. She opened her mouth to say something, but Doc motioned to Laura with his head. Sarah nodded and walked haltingly to her son. Laura made an effort to step aside but Scott pulled her back to his side.

"Luke, I'm so sorry. I've really made a mess of things. I've wanted to tell you for so long about your father and me, but I just couldn't bring myself to do it. Whatever image you had of me, I didn't want to destroy it. As for your father, I figured after all these years, you'd just forget about it."

"How could I forget? I couldn't stand not knowing what really happened, and you'd never talk about it. Now I guess I found out more than I wanted to know."

"Like those awful things Sam said, I . . ."

Luke put his hand over his mother's mouth. "I'm not interested in anything that polecat said. He was an evil man. Whatever happened, it's over. So, let's just get the hell out of here."

While Luke and Sarah embraced, Laura sidled up to Doc. "You just couldn't let him do it could you?"

"What are you talking about, child?"

"Kill his own father. That would be a terrible thing for him to live with."

"Nonsense, I didn't do that for him. I did it for Abigail. You're not the only one who loved her, you know."

"I know," she murmured. "I've known it for a long time."

Doc held her at arm's length. "It's something I should have done a long time ago. Somehow I felt responsible for her . . ."

"No, Doc," Laura interrupted, "Hardin was responsible. He

was a wicked man who got what he deserved. If it hadn't been you, it would have been Scott, I mean Luke, except you couldn't stand by and let him kill his own father?"

"That's nonsense. Sam Hardin couldn't have fathered Luke, or anybody else for that matter."

Laura studied Doc through dubious eyes. "What makes you so sure?"

"The sonnuva bitch was sterile."

Laura looked deep into Doc's eyes. "This is important to me, Doc. Don't lie to me. You're saying Sam Hardin was not Luke's father, right?"

Doc returned her gaze without flinching. "Impossible. Sam Hardin knew he was sterile. I'm the one who told him. He suspected that Abigail was seeing someone, and in his twisted logic assumed it was Jesse, but Sam was a coward, too much of a coward to confront Jesse. That made him hate Jesse all the more."

Laura threw her arms around his neck and kissed him on the cheek. "You don't know how much that means to me."

"Oh, I have an idea," he said his pale blue eyes twinkling. "So, what are you going to do about this feller, Scott, uh, Luke, now that we don't have Hardin to worry about any more?"

"You leave that to me," she said with an impish grin.

Doc walked over to Sarah and examined her face. "Are you all right? Did Hardin . . . I mean did he . . .?"

Sarah gave Doc a tight squeeze. "Nothing happened. He just knocked me around a little, but I'm all right. By the way, thanks for being my hero. I really think Sam would have shot me."

"I have absolutely no doubt about that. He was crazy enough to do it."

"One more thing, Doc. What you just told Laura about Sam, is it true?"

Doc nodded, "Every word of it."

"Are you absolutely sure? I mean you're not just making this up for Luke's sake or for mine, are you?"

"If Sam Hardin were Luke's father, nothing would have suited me more than to have his own son send him to boot hill. Would've served him right."

At that moment Billy came from around the building with the reins to Sam Hardin's horse in one hand and Scott's Winchester in the other. Sarah stared at this new member of the party until recognition set in. She broke away from Doc and ran to him. "Oh my God, Billy . . . Billy Bear Heart. Where did you come from? What are you doing here? Where were you when all the ruckus was going on?"

"That's another long story, ma'am. As for your second question, I came in through the back door, and had this rifle trained on Hardin's head all the while he was running off at the mouth. Doc, here, was one split second ahead, or it would've been me who done him in."

Sarah hugged him tightly and said, "Billy, you were always so protective of Luke. You were the big brother he never had."

"How about big cousin?"

Sarah gave him a perplexed look. "Big cousin?"

Billy glanced at Luke and made a questioning gesture. Luke shrugged as if to say, "What the hell, all the other cats are out the bag."

"Mrs. Chandler, brace yourself for this. Your uncle, Don Lucas Fernando Martinez, is my father. Now what do you think of that?"

Sarah put both hands to her head. "My God, is there anything else I should know before we go back to town?"

"Well, there are a few things," Luke broke in, "but they can wait. We'll catch you up on them at Teresa's. In the meantime, what do we do with Hardin?"

Doc walked over to where Hardin lay, bent down to feel for a pulse and made a pronouncement. "I officially declare Samuel Hardin dead. Cause of death, a single shot to the head in self-defense, brought on by his own greed and arrogance. Throw the sonnuva bitch on the buckboard and let's head back to town. Sarah, you ride with me in the buggy."

"Laura," Doc said, "I reckon that knocks you out of a seat, so you have two choices . . . walk back or ride Hardin's horse and keep Luke company on the way back."

Laura winked at Doc. "He's going to be stuck with me a lot longer than that."

Chapter Thirty-Five

It wasn't meant to be a funeral procession, but that's what it turned out to be. With Laura, Billy, and Luke in the lead on horseback followed by Sarah and Doc in the buggy. The buckboard clattered across the railroad tracks on its way to the establishment of James Caldwell, master carpenter and casket maker. By the time the cortege reached Caldwell's place, the body wrapped in Sarah's Indian blanket was the object of intense curiosity. It didn't take long for word to get around and in no time at all the street filled with people, curious as to the identity of the mystery corpse. They pushed and shoved as they closed in on the buckboard, showing little respect for the dead.

Jake pulled up in front of Caldwell's and handed the reins to Teresa. "As soon as I unload the body, you take the wagon to the stable. I'll catch up with all of you at the house."

Jake hefted Sam Hardin's body and draped it over his shoulder as if it were a side of beef. As soon as Teresa pulled away, everyone crowded around him wanting to know who was wrapped in the blanket.

"Hey, Jake, who's the stiff?"

"What's the big mystery?"

"How come Laura's riding Sam Hardin's horse?"

"Is that Hardin you bringing in?"

It took just one look at Jake's scowling face for them to shut their yaps and open a path to Caldwell's front door. As soon as Jake was inside, Caldwell closed the door and drew the curtain over the front windows.

Jake dumped the body on a table and Caldwell asked, "Who bought a ticket to boot hill this time?"

"Sam Hardin."

Caldwell whistled through his teeth. "That Scott Martin sure has left his mark on this town."

"This isn't his doing, but never mind that. I'd appreciate your nailing the lid on this casket right away. He's got part of his head blown off and it ain't a pretty sight."

"I don't guess it's any of my business how it got that way, is it?"

"You'll find out soon enough. For the moment, let's just say he shouldn't have been standing where he was when the bullet showed up."

"Humph, you could say the same thing about Marv lying in

that coffin over there. Was just about fixing to bury him. I reckon I'll make it a double funeral."

Jake pondered that for a moment. "Good idea, James. Wait until four o'clock and pass the word to that crowd outside that Sarah Chandler's got a few things she wants to say. In the meantime, I'll go hunt up the marshal and explain what happened."

"Don't bother. Him and his deputy left this morning with Snake."

"Hmm, that's too bad . . . too bad for Snake, that is. If he knew Hardin was dead, he'd keep his trap shut. Now he's going to talk his fool head off hoping to get a lighter sentence."

Jake chuckled quietly and started for the front door. Halfway there he changed his mind. "I believe I'm gonna slip out the back. I ain't up to dealing with that mob right now. Be sure and tell 'em to be at the bone yard at four. And you might as well tell 'em it's Sam in the box. When they hear that, they'll show up for sure."

•　　•　　•　　•　　•

By the time Jake walked back to his house, the others had gathered around the kitchen table. In the aftermath of the morning's drama, the atmosphere was subdued. The ladies quietly sipped the tea Teresa had prepared while the men "medicated" themselves with some of Doc Carver's "full bodied elixir."

Teresa studied Sarah's swollen lip that matched the purple bruise on her forehead. "So, Doc," Teresa said, "what about Sarah? Is she going to be all right?"

"No major damage. She'll be OK, but she should take it easy for a few days."

"I'll have plenty of time to rest. Right now there are some questions I want answered. Starting with you, Luke. Whatever possessed you to come here, and why didn't you tell me?"

Luke shrugged wearily. "I think we've already covered that. Why don't we just let the past be the past? Maybe when the shock and emotions have passed, we can talk about it more calmly. This much I do know, however, I found out what I was looking for."

Sarah stared at her hands. "And probably a lot more than you bargained for."

Luke removed the letter from his shirt pocket. "Not only about you, but about Pa and Billy as well, but, before I go into that, I have a letter for you. It's from Pa."

Sarah's eyes grew wide and her hand shook as she took the letter from Luke. "You've seen him?"

Luke shook his head. "I've seen his grave."

"His grave? That means he's . . . but when . . . how did you get the letter?"

"Shortly after Pa was shot, he showed up at a mission just outside of Santa Fe where Billy's mother was living. She was the first one to reach him when he fell off his horse. He gave it to her right before he died and asked her to get it to you."

Sarah looked to Billy. "And it took all this time?"

"She didn't know who you were or where to locate you. There was no address on the envelope, just your name, so she just held on to it. I didn't know she was my mother until shortly before Luke got back. When I got word that Luke was in Whiskey River, I rode in to meet him and we ended up in Santa Fe two days later. When I told my mother who he was, she made the connection."

Sarah turned back to Luke. "Is there anything else I ought to know?"

"Just one more thing, the land is yours. Hardin took it illegally, and just about everybody here is part of the conspiracy. He gave them each two hundred acres to keep quiet, and as long as they kept their mouths shut, they got to hang on to their land."

"My God," Sarah said, "no wonder they don't put out the welcome mat for strangers, and it's no mystery why they were so upset at my coming back here. They must have been afraid I was going to boot them off that land."

"Which you can legally do, since it never belonged to Sam

Hardin in the first place," Luke added, "but as your lawyer, I wouldn't advise it. However, before I get into that, I think you should read the letter."

Sarah turned the envelope over in her hands, slipped her finger under the flap, and then stopped. "No," she said, "first I want to say a few things. Sam said some horrible things this morning and I want you to know the truth. We did have a romance going for a while. But that was all it was, a silly crush. I never had any feelings for him. Jesse was a good man . . . kind, generous, hardworking, but definitely not romantic. I finally came to my senses and broke it off, but Sam couldn't deal with that. He started pestering me, wouldn't leave me alone. At first it was innocent pleading, trying to persuade me to resume our little romance. Then it became vicious. I couldn't convince him it was over.

This went on for six years and I couldn't decide if I should tell Jesse and if I did, what he would do. Then Sam threatened to tell Jesse about our affair and that you were his son. I couldn't bear doing that to Jesse. I had enough guilt as it was, so I just picked up and left with you and Billy."

Sarah stared at the envelope again and said, "Whatever's in here is between Jesse and me. Now I'm going to my room, and after I read Jesse's letter, I'm going to think about what I'm going to say to these dear sweet people of Whiskey River. If you'll excuse me."

Sarah, alone in her room, settled in the rocking chair next to the bed. Each time she started to open the envelope she stopped short and turned it over and over and then pressed it to her breast.

Dear God, isn't it enough I was unfaithful to him, that I took his only child away from him and drove him to gamble and drink? Haven't you punished me enough? Do I really need to hear what a tramp I am from the man I walked out on? I already know that. Why are you doing this to me?

Sarah, no longer able to evade the inevitable, ripped open the envelope and removed the letter. Without hesitation she unfolded it and began to read.

"April 9, 1861

My Dear Sarah,

I hope this letter finds you and the boys well. I've had a lot of time to think about us and there are a few things I want to say that I hope will help you understand what has happened between us.

When you told me you were pregnant, I wasn't sure it was my child. After all, our moments of intimacy were far and few between. I know now that I should have given you the chance to explain, but I was too hurt and angry. I have come to understand, however, it's I who is to blame. It took me all this while to realize how much I love you and need you. Can you ever forgive me for driving you away?

Please come back. This will go out on tomorrow's stagecoach. Let me know your answer as soon as you receive it.

All my love, Jesse"

When Sarah had finished, her tears fell on the paper in torrents turning the ink into unreadable splotches. She stared in dismay at the date that was still legible.

Luke said he died on August 16 and this is dated April 9. Good heavens, he carried this letter around for over three months. Oh, Jesse, why didn't you mail it when you said you were going to? Didn't you know I would have come immediately? You'd still be alive today.

Chapter Thirty-Six

There's probably no real good day for a burial, but as days go, this wasn't a bad one. The bright sun played hide and seek behind fleecy clouds, while the crisp afternoon breeze scattered the leaves from the sycamores and oaks that dotted the hillside. Autumn and the winter that would follow weren't far away. When the Chandler entourage arrived, most everybody else from Whiskey River had gathered, more out of curiosity than to mourn Hardin's passing. They immediately split up into groups . . . us and them.

James Caldwell, shovel in hand, stood over the two coffins he had already lowered into the grave. Eager to get it over with he said, "Anyone like to say a few words?"

There were a few nervous coughs and several people shuffled their feet, but no one came forward. Finally Fred Henderson cleared his throat and said nervously, "We're here 'cause Caldwell said Sarah Chandler had something to say to us."

Luke Chandler stepped forward.

"That's right, but before she does, there are a few things I want to say. This isn't my first time in Whiskey River. I was here about fifteen years ago, but back then I was known as Luke Chandler."

Luke waited for the murmuring to subside before he continued. "I returned over two weeks ago to find out what happened to my father, Jesse Chandler. During that time, I was insulted, assaulted and nearly killed, but that didn't stop me from finding out the truth. And the truth is . . . Sam Hardin paid Snake Weston five hundred dollars to shoot my father. He illegally took over my mother's land, and everyone one of you made a pact to keep quiet about it in return for a piece of the pie."

"There was nothing illegal about it," Ed Gladstone shouted. "Sam Hardin rightfully took that land in payment of Jesse's gambling debts. That land is legally ours."

"That's right," Tom Perkins yelled. "It's all legal and proper, so pack up and go back where you came from."

Luke motioned for them to be quiet. "I'll tell you what else is the truth. In Santa Fe I confirmed that the land is still officially recorded in the name of Mrs. Sarah Martinez Chandler. As far as the law is concerned that property is still hers, which means all of you are trespassing on her land."

An anonymous voice shouted. "You can't take it away from us. We've been living on that land for over fourteen years now."

"That's not my place to say. I'll leave that up Sarah Chandler, but right now I'd like to say a few words about two people we're burying today. Sam Hardin was an evil man. I doubt if anyone here will mourn his passing. His greed and lust for power drove him to kill one of the finest men this territory has ever known, and when his widow, Sarah Chandler, showed up unexpectedly, he followed her and took her forcibly to one of his line shacks. We tracked him there where he was holding her at gunpoint. When he saw that we weren't going to back off and realized there was no other way out, he was done in by his own gun."

Doc and Laura exchanged incredulous looks. Jake and Teresa chuckled quietly, while Billy and Sarah's eyes rolled back in their heads.

"Sam Hardin wasn't the kind to take his own life," someone shouted.

Luke held up Sam Hardin's Derringer. "This is the gun that killed him. His name is engraved on it right here. Everybody who knew Hardin knows that he was left-handed. Ask James Caldwell if there isn't a single bullet hole in his left temple."

All heads turned toward Caldwell who nodded his agreement.

"How do we know you didn't hunt him down like an animal and make it look like he committed suicide?"

"It's a simple matter of fact," Luke said. "We've got six witnesses. They'll all testify to what I just said. I believe you all know how that works, don't you?"

When the buzzing and murmuring abated, Luke said, "Now as to Marv, I doubt if any of us gathered here will shed a tear for him. Say what you want, though, he may not have been too bright, and he hung out with a real bad hombre, but at least he wasn't two faced. Don't know if that's enough to make up for all the bad things he did in his life, so all we can ask is that the Lord have mercy on his soul. Now, Sarah has a few words to say."

The crowd fell silent as Sarah stepped forward. She deliberately looked at those who once were her friends. Those who didn't avoid her gaze, wilted under her glare.

"I had my reasons for leaving here, none of which are any business of yours. And, it's likewise none of your business why I came back. All you have to know is this. I hold every one of you just as responsible for taking my husband away and trying to strip me of my property. From the moment I returned, you tried to drive me away. Well, I've got some bad news for you . . . I am back for good and I'm taking immediate possession of my property."

While they were still in shock, Sarah motioned for Billy to join her. "I want you to meet Billy Bear Heart. He went back East with us when I left. I didn't know it then, but I just learned he and I are kin. His mother is a Navajo Indian and his father is . . . (Sarah paused to suppress a smile at all the shocked looks) my uncle, Lucas Fernando Martinez, who left me all this property. You better get used to seeing Billy around because he is the new foreman of what used to be the Lazy-H."

Billy said nothing, but his body language said, "Huh?"

Sarah glanced in Billy's direction. "Aren't you going to say something, Billy?"

Billy broke out in a huge grin. "It's good to be back home."

At first, the gathering was too stunned to speak, but when they finally found their voices, they reacted as if Geronimo and his war party had suddenly appeared brandishing scalping knives.

When they had quieted down, Sarah continued, "Now, here's what's going to happen. I am transferring ownership of all the land that you are presently occupying to Billy. In return Billy will write a will that leaves those parcels to the present occupants, or their heirs, upon his death, at which time they will receive a clear title. That means as long as Billy is alive, the land belongs to him. However, if Billy should happen to die from anything but natural causes, the will automatically becomes null and void and all property in question reverts to me. I'm sure that will make Billy's well being a matter of utmost concern to all of you."

"You can't get away with that," Tom Perkins shouted. "Indians can't own property."

Sarah smiled indulgently. "I don't know if that's true, but it really doesn't make any difference. You see, the land you all are squatting on represents about half of the entire estate. Now, Billy is half Indian and half white, and it's his white half that will own the land, but that's not the real issue. Whiskey River used to be a decent place to live, where everybody got along. There's no reason it can't be like that again, if we simply put aside everything that's gone on these past fifteen years. Besides, I think it's about time the white man and the Indian learned how to live together in peace, don't you?"

Doc took a pint bottle of whiskey from his pocket and held it high. "I'll drink to that."

Jake and Teresa hugged each other and laughed like kids. "Welcome home Sarah."

Fred and Mary Henderson were the first to "cross the line." After an awkward silence, Fred said, "Welcome back, Sarah. We're truly sorry about Jesse, and about what took place here . . . well, I guess we should be ashamed. We weren't part of it, but we did know what was going on. Hope you can forgive us," and hastily retreated.

Slowly and painfully the others joined the Hendersons in expressing their embarrassment and guilt, except the Perkins and the Gladstones who departed in a huff.

Sarah called after them, "Marjorie, Hester, I would especially like a word with you two."

They spun around to face Sarah.

"Well aren't you the self-righteous one? We have nothing to say to you." Hester Gladstone snapped.

Sarah nodded. "You don't have to say anything, just listen. I can understand how you feel. How do you imagine I felt when I learned that Sam Hardin had snatched my land away from me? Or how I felt when I learned that so many of you I considered my friends betrayed that friendship?

But, I haven't come back for revenge. I only ask that you look into your own hearts and accept responsibility for your actions. After all, you were willing accomplices."

"Accomplice to what?" Hester spat.

Marjorie, who had been silent up to this point, piped up, "For God's sake, Hester, you know darn well what Sarah's talking about. Admit it, we all knew what we were doing."

Marjorie stuck out her hand and met Sarah's eyes. "It was wrong what we did and we're sorry. Please forgive us."

Sarah took the hand and said, "Of course I do"

She looked over Marjorie's shoulder at Hester, whose face was purple with rage. "I have nothing more to say to you, Sarah, and as far as taking land that some half-breed leaves me in his will, you can forget it."

Sarah shrugged. "In that case, Hester, Luke will work out a settlement for the improvements you made on the property, and I'll expect you to be off it in one month."

Doc raised his bottle. "I'll drink to that."

Laura spun Luke around and said, "Well, what are you waiting for? Are you going to kiss me or am I going to have to throw you down and hog-tie you?"

After some thought Luke said, "Why don't you throw me down and we'll see where it goes from there?"

"Uh, unh, we'll see where it goes from here."

Luke cocked his head and replied, "You know . . . I think I'd really like to open a law practice in Santa Fe. One day this territory is going to be a state and I'm sure there's a *señorita* there who'd like to be the first governor's wife."

This time Luke was ready for the left hook. He caught her arm, spun her around and pulled her close. Right before he kissed her he said, "You're going to have to learn to behave more properly if you're going to be the first governor's wife."

Laura giggled, "Only in public your governorship."

Made in the USA
Charleston, SC
20 April 2016